I0445424

FIGHTING OUT OF NEW MILFORD, USA

GB Hope

Fighting Out of New Milford, USA

A work of fiction by GB Hope ©

Published by Bronwyn Editions UK 2013

www.bronwyneditions.co.uk

ISBN: 978–0-9570745-3-8

Cover design by Jon Parris

Printed by Lightning Source UK 2013

A copy of this book has been sent to the British Library for legal deposit

Fighting Out of New Milford, USA

By the same author:

Who Do You Think *You* Are? You're My Henry Allbones

Queen of Spades

Stranger on Stranger

The Genie-alogy of Nathan Levy

Fighting Out of Mobberley, England

4

GB Hope

Dedication

For P
In your next life,
when you find yourself as an English boy at university,
watch for the arrival of the cute American girl... that'll be me.

Acknowledgement

To the girls of San Diego

GB Hope

FIGHTING OUT OF NEW MILFORD, USA

PROLOGUE

It had been a bitch of a job positioning the Gatling gun, while still on its carriage, on the rear footplate of the Wild West train. They had wanted to remove the wheels, place it on a tripod, but no, the New York lawyers and the suits from London had been insistent – the whole thing must go on as it was. It had been winched on with millimetres to spare, then bolted down. A real, thoroughgoing, bitch of a job.

Now, the two elderly engineers in their blue overalls and blue caps, one with a magnificent twirly white moustache, stood behind the 1874 brass and steel model, giddy as children. They were ready for a test firing. The lawyers and suits had retired to a safe viewing platform, fifty yards further up the track.

'Are we ready?' asked George: the one with the moustache.

'We're ready,' said Jim, polishing the brass stock one last time.

George started to crank the handle and bullets began spewing out along the track. He moved in an arc, left, then right, sharing in Jim's delighted laughter. George increased his speed, firing faster. It was an astonishing sight as the bullets started to rip to shreds the robotic zombies which had been aimlessly wandering around for the last three hours behind a wire fence. Bullets shredded through clothing and took off heads and arms. The air was full of dust and smoke and bits of synthetic rubber.

George only stopped when the ammunition ran out. He looked at Jim, and Jim looked at him – that had been worth all the effort.

ONE

As the man bled from a head wound, half in and half out of his rental car, he was surprised how clearly he was aware that it had been a gun barrel that had bushwhacked him, and that his attacker was wearing a dirty Chicago Bears sweatshirt and even dirtier jeans.

With one hand propping himself up off the floor, he checked his cheekbone with the other – not broken, he believed, but hurting like hell and already starting to swell. He looked up just as the barrel of the pistol came to press against his forehead. The gun was held sideways, like in the movies, and the stupidity of it actually caused the man to laugh, until pain made him stop.

'Excuse me, mate,' he said in an English accent. 'I've been mugged before. Once in London, which is to be expected, and once in Oxford, which I have to tell you was a total surprise. Anyway, they at least had the good manners to let me get out of the bloody car first!'

It was an alleyway, at dusk, near to the restaurant the

Englishman had been trying to get to after remembering a favourite old episode of *Man vs. Food,* while stuck in his hovel of a Chicago hotel room. The young attacker stepped back, maybe out of surprise, or with some modicum of criminal gallantry. The gun remained aimed sideways.

'You're a white guy,' pointed out the Englishman, as he managed to stand.

'Why be a racist?'

'They told me not to come here. That it was a rough, black area.'

'Every place is bad these days.'

'What's your name?'

'Fuck my name. Let's move this on, man.'

'I haven't got any cash.'

'Cash ain't no good anyway. I want those rings.'

'You want my Superbowl rings?'

'They ain't no Superbowl rings. Stop joking. I'm deadly serious.'

'I suppose you can have the rings. They only remind me of wives number one and two. I'm still friends with number three, by the way, but that's a long story. Do you need anything else? You look a little hungry, if you don't mind me saying so.'

'You're a crazy son of a bitch. What are you, man, Welsh?'

'Welsh? Fucking Welsh! I'm a Brummie, mate. Birmingham.'

'Sorry, didn't mean to cause no offence.'

'What are you, Canadian?'

The youth with the gun laughed. 'What the hell,' he said, looking resigned to the banter. 'I'm from Minnesota, but in Chicago when the shit went down, and I heard my home town's gone, so stayed here.'

'You've been here two years? Have you been home?'

The youth scratched a sore on his neck, considering whether to keep talking. 'No, my brother made it here. No one else survived.'

'I'm sorry. I really am. Anyway, shall we get back to the mugging?'

'It's not supposed to be like this. Are you stalling for cops? Because if you are, you'll have a long wait.'

'No, no.' The Englishman handed over the rings. 'Seriously, come and have something to eat. You look famished.'

'Are you some kind of pervert?'

The Englishman feigned giving that a lot of thought. 'You perhaps think that's why my wives left me?'

There was a stand-off in the gloom. Finally, the youth from Minnesota shrugged his shoulders – it was a mad, mad world now – rob a man and he offers to buy you dinner.

They walked towards the restaurant. The gun was tucked into the youth's belt at the back, under the sweatshirt. The Englishman had been warned not to try anything. He had a handkerchief pressed against his face. The bleeding had stopped, but he had a feeling that was not altogether a good sign.

They sat facing each other in a red leather booth, ordered chicken wings, cheese burgers and shakes and ice cubes in a towel, *if you'd be so kind.* The waitress hadn't batted an eye, either at the injury or the scruffiness of the younger man.

Sipping their drinks, while they waited for the food, they could look at each other properly for the first time. The young American would be handsome without the haunted expression he carried with him. He wore a crew cut and a week's growth of dark beard. He was eighteen. The Englishman was in his best suit, pleased that his blood had only ruined his white shirt. He was nearing forty. He was still happily married to wife number three back in Wolverhampton (near Birmingham, UK – that city was still a mess after the riots and not safe to live in), but he couldn't help spinning a tale when the chance presented itself.

'I'm Kevin,' said the Englishman.

'I'm Kevin too,' said the American.

'Oh, are you? Well, I'll be Kev.'

'No, I'm Kev.'

'Okay. You be Kev. Christ, we could be here all night at this rate.'

They shook hands over the table.

'Kev, you're from Minnesota, you say, but you're wearing a Chicago Bears top.'

'Clothing's just clothing these days.'

'That's fair enough.'

Their chicken wings and ice in a towel arrived. Kevin tended to his face and left the appetiser all to Kev.

Blackpool Tower came down in the riots of 2016. It burned for six days before crashing across the promenade into the Irish sea. For the survivors in Lancashire and the North-West of England, in particular, it symbolised the madness and tragedy of those terrible few months.

It had been a northern hemisphere phenomenon. Some said the collapse of the banks caused it, others the complete and sudden end to fuel supplies. Casualties were still being counted. No one was being prosecuted for murder because the justice system was down. In most of the UK, martial law was only just being replaced by the rebuilt police force. As in America, cash didn't exist any more, everything was bought and sold on Government vouchers. The people were trying to get back to normal. It was almost like after the Great War, with no family left untouched, the only difference being that the cataclysm had taken place on British soil and, at a rough estimate, destroyed forty per cent of the housing stock in every city, every town and every village. Of course, by some strange twist of fate, a few places escaped untouched, little places where everyone knew everybody else, where there weren't too many furious youths or disaffected underclass: little places like Leverton in Lincolnshire, or St Ives in Cornwall, or Buxton in Derbyshire.

Blackpool was not so lucky. When the electricity was off

for forty-eight hours straight, the gangs were on the streets. Then the cash machines stopped being filled up, and the petrol stations were left to run dry. Nobody could go anywhere, do anything, buy anything. Looting came naturally, followed by violence. The police were quickly overwhelmed. It was the same pattern almost everywhere – the government's worst nightmare. Murder came straight after the looting. But because the situation couldn't be contained, it went on for weeks and became mass slaughter.

Jon Armstrong got through it fairly unscathed. He did lose a girlfriend, but all his family survived. That was down in London, where he used to be a cocky Private Investigator, driving an Aston Martin and living the high life. He was still a PI, but his firm had been burned out of The Strand, so he worked from home, and now drove a more sensible ten-year-old Land Rover. He was back in Blackpool and had mixed feelings about it. Two and a half years earlier he had been sent north, to Liverpool, actually, in search of people who fitted into a certain criteria to take part in a social experiment. In other words, he'd been adding to a group of people who went into a locked-down shopping mall in Berkshire for six months, pretending to be hiding from a zombie apocalypse. The mixed bunch, which included his two finds (he'd failed on his third attempt) of Lee from Liverpool and Leila from Blackpool, were all paid £100,000 to take part. Ironic that when they got out, the money was worthless and they walked into an apocalypse for real.

He never really knew what went on in that mall for six months. Ex-colleagues had talked about divisions forming and violence flaring near the end. The man who had set it up, billionaire Michael Hester, hadn't made it out, apparently. But there were no police to investigate it, and the mall was still closed to the public, its contents rotting away. Jon had no knowledge of what had become of Lee, but he knew Leila had survived. Now he was to find her again, and he felt terribly guilty about it.

He drove north on the almost empty motorways, having glimpses of devastation and efforts to rebuild. He paid for his fuel ration with UK government vouchers and ate the packed lunch his mother had prepared for him. He was twenty-eight years old.

In Blackpool, Leila's previous address no longer existed. She had been a sixteen-year-old foster child back then, a little minx, as he remembered, of Middle Eastern descent, lovely but damaged, shy but promiscuous with the local boys. She had stayed at his flat prior to going into the mall, and had offered sex at one stage. He had politely declined.

He sat in his Land Rover looking at the angry sea and wondered what Leila was like now. He believed she was back in Blackpool; he really wanted to see her again.

Kevin paid for their meal with US government vouchers and they stepped out of the restaurant.

'Now, where were we?' asked Kevin. 'Oh, yes, you were in

the process of mugging me.'

'How's your face?'

'A frozen mask.'

'Listen, my name's not really Kev. I was just kidding you along. It's Leland. There's a doctor lives in my building. Come back with me and I'll get him to see you.'

'Come back to your building with you? Are you some kind of pervert, Leland?'

Leland laughed. Then he handed back Kevin's rings as they headed to the rental car.

'What the fuck are you doing in Chicago?' asked Leland.

'I'm looking for people.'

Leland shook his head. 'You just get crazier and crazier.'

They drove to Leland's run down apartment building. It wasn't visible at night, but the roof had been lost to fire. Leland led them up to the second floor where he banged on a door. Kevin imagined the big eye looking through the peephole, then the door was opened by a middle-aged white man wearing decent shirt and trousers. A woman peered out nervously from further inside the apartment.

'Doc,' said Leland. 'This here's my friend Kevin. He's hurt himself.'

They were ushered in as if the East German secret police were monitoring the hallway. The Doc smiled reassuringly at his wife, waved her away and made Kevin sit down on a chair in the kitchen part of the small apartment.

'I'm Doctor Holloway.'

'Kevin Reed.'

'What's hit you, Mr Reed?'

Kevin pointed slowly at Leland. 'Him.'

The Doc glanced at Leland, not appearing surprised. He assessed the damage to Kevin's face, then went to fetch his medical bag.

20

GB Hope

TWO

English couple, Lee and Claudia, sat on the floor of his makeshift martial arts dojang in New Milford, Connecticut, while he waited for his students to get changed next door. He was in his white dobok uniform with his black belt around his waist, stretching his groin out by pressing his knees to the side. She was in a thick woollen dress and woollen leggings, her boots off, of course, huddled close to him in the cold room. He nuzzled in under her wild winter-style brunette hair and kissed her pale cheek. They were very much in love.

'You know what, babe,' he said. 'The world went to hell in a handcart two years ago but I'm still getting fat Americans coming in here.'

She grinned, kissed him on the mouth and made a move. 'I love that one who always looks like he's having a heart attack and says "I wasn't born for this shit!" when you make them run round the room. Right, I'll get some groceries in. Have a good lesson. Do you want anything?'

'See if they've started selling popcorn again.'

'Proper food, I meant.'

He watched her leave. He laughed when she turned at the door and made a big show of bowing to the room.

During that bizarre six-month social experiment in the Berkshire shopping mall, Lee and Leila from Blackpool had been an item, until near the end where she decided she no longer wanted a boyfriend and moved him on to fellow mall-mate, Claudia – it seemed a normal thing to do at the time.

The zombie apocalypse game had been interesting all round. Friendships were made, Lee liked being with Leila very much, but he and Claudia should have been the real deal from the start. There were divisions in there also: normal problems between people which were magnified in the surreal world inside the mall and, by the end, there were two separate groups living apart in different areas of the vast building. It all came down to the orchestrator of the whole event, Michael Hester, with more money than sense, wanting to establish communes in the US as he realised the world was heading for the toilet. He set up the Berkshire internment as a dry-run, picking a varied selection of companions to see how they dealt with it. Unfortunately, he fixated on making Leila and Claudia prime candidates for joining his new harem. They weren't too keen, so looked to Lee's group for protection. In the final weeks inside, everything deteriorated into paranoid hostility and ultimately into violence. Lee had had to kill to protect Leila and Claudia, not Hester, but a couple of his new lieutenants. Leila's brother, finally tracking her down, had taken care of Hester. Then they all ventured out into the unfolding horror of the breakdown of normal society. They went their separate ways.

Lee and Claudia stayed together. First they managed to get to Claudia's home city of York to look for her parents. The riots had happened there, but not to the insane levels of other places. They found Claudia's home to be one of the burned-out wrecks. Surviving neighbours broke the news to Claudia that her parents were both dead.

Claudia had other relatives in Yorkshire, but Lee was her family from that point on. They stole a motorbike and made it to the Cheshire village of Mobberley. They didn't find any living neighbours to buffer them from the horror. Instead they came across Lee's dead mother and stepfather. Lee buried them that night in the back garden.

Lee didn't know where his real father was. They managed to find his sister and her husband living in Manchester and stayed with them for a few months.

Then Claudia suggested Connecticut. It took him a few minutes to realise it was actually a state in America she was talking about, then he heard her out about her American cousins – men and women who were ex-military and who went out into the woods with hunting rifles and the orange clothing, but still managed to shoot each other no doubt. They were people perfectly attuned for the rebuilding time ahead. Plus, Connecticut had missed most of the trouble, unlike New York and great swathes of the Eastern Seaboard. Lee agreed, they planned, then quickly realised that there was no longer anything in place such as passports or visas, and booked passage on a container ship bound for New Jersey.

Claudia put on her boots and coat and cycled from the dojang on Railway Street along almost traffic-free roads, to the store on Main Street. From there it was a short ride to the apartment they lived in for free, in exchange for working in her cousin's bakery. Claudia said hello to the girls in the store. She loved New Milford, especially the Housatonic river which she and Lee often walked alongside. It was not, though, what she had expected of her life, when she dreamed as a teenager of winning something like *The X-Factor* and having an American home in The Hamptons or Malibu Beach. But the people were good there in Connecticut and she was settled. Maybe, in a couple of years, they could move on. Lee had once told her of a desire to do the Route 66 journey, before all the trouble, but back in those days he had been too poor to do it anyway.

Claudia picked up the supplies she needed and headed home. Their apartment was small but tidy, with a balcony they appreciated in the summer. Electricity was now almost always reliable, but there was only radio, no cable or TV. They lived in the one room, with a sleeping area that had a mattress on the floor – Japanese style, Lee kidded her. In the living area there were a few photos of her parents, but none of Lee's. A big rug covered the bare floorboards, and on the wall hung a

Leeds United FC flag which used to belong to her brother. Apart from that it was very minimalist, but she was happy with Lee there.

She would cook pasta, she decided, Lee being ravenous after one of his lessons. Lee's father had been the real martial artist, teaching all over the world. Perhaps that had added to the family breakdown – she knew Lee had never really been able to communicate properly with his father. Naturally he had become involved himself in the sport, principally Tae Kwon-Do, but later moving into mixed-martial arts and competing in a few cage fights. She smiled as she looked out of the window, thinking about her loveable Lee in one of those brutal match-ups. The first time he had defended her honour had been in the shopping mall when that man from Manchester had attempted to assault her. All the group had gathered, accusations had flown back and forth, then when the man had made an aggressive move towards her – bang! In a flash Lee swept his legs from under him, had him in a death hold around the neck, and had to be prised away. Claudia's smile faded as the time in the mall came back to her in little flashbacks. Lee had ended up killing that idiot from Manchester. But that was a long time ago in a completely different world.

A man by the name of Andy Ding stopped at a diner on route seven, close to his final destination of New Milford. Over an omelette, hash browns and coffee, he re-read his instructions from the New York office. He leafed through his thin manila folder, revealing images of both Lee and Claudia with their particulars underneath. He was completely clear in his mind about those two, so he flicked to his other three targets. He was to find a retired widower, preferably a man of standing in his community, an ex-Government official or teacher, perhaps. Andy was a man of few facial expressions but that element of his task brought a little shake of the head. His next target was to collect a handsome male teenager, a boy-band look-alike, preferably without close family ties, perhaps a foreigner, an illegal alien if possible. He had attempted that job three times already before leaving New York and almost been arrested twice. Lastly, there was a mature female – apparently he had carte blanche on that one.

He looked around the diner, more in hope than expectation, but all the other customers were useless for his requirements. He pushed his plate away from him and drank his coffee. He looked through the window at the cold day. A few trucks went by on the road. His journey up from New York had been very uneventful; few people drove unless they had to these days. He looked at his dusty 5-series BMW sitting out there, immediately seeing the right front puncture. He signalled the waitress for the check.

'Do you know where the nearest garage is?' he asked the waitress when she finally came over.

'Sorry, no idea.'

Andy thought that sounded like "this ain't no information

bureau, mister". He paid with vouchers and went out to the car. He knew there was no spare wheel so just drove on. He found a place quite soon, thinking the waitress must have known about it all along. Maybe she didn't care for his Asian appearance. As he pulled onto the garage forecourt he thought about going back there and discussing it with her, but immediately dismissed the idea. What was the point?

Business was slow; he had to go inside to find someone for help, calling out as he did so. From underneath a Ford Focus up on a ramp appeared Simon Cowell's dream contestant. The kid was blond, very good-looking, with an obviously athletic build, even in dirty blue overalls. The face was a little bit sullen.

'What can I help you with?' came out with a Scandinavian tone.

'I've got a flat.'

'Let's have a look.'

Not quite the personality of a pop star, thought Andy, as he followed the mechanic back out front.

While the blond mechanic fixed the puncture, Andy wandered away slightly to have a cigarette. He came back when he heard the nuts being locked with the pressure gun.

'How far to New Milford?' he asked.

'It's about another ten miles.'

'Is that accent Norwegian?'

'Swedish.'

'Swedish, yeah?'

Over in Chicago, Kevin the Brummie Reed woke up in Leland's bed. Leland had spent the night on the sofa, the least he could do after trying to cave in the Englishman's skull. Now there was pain: terrible, serious pain that tried to stop him getting up, but he was hungry and cold. He still had his trousers on but had swapped his bloodied shirt for a sweater the doctor's wife had given him. He found his feet, found his painkillers, and went to the bathroom for water to take two tablets with. In the bathroom mirror he saw that he looked like he had fallen three floors onto concrete.

Through to the living/dining area of Leland's apartment, Leland was there making coffee. 'Good morning. How do you take your coffee?'

'Alongside a plate of bacon and eggs.'

'I've no food in. We'll eat out. My treat.'

Kevin took his offered coffee mug and sat down in front of a dead wide screen television. He thought Leland's treat would stretch to the local garbage cans, but he held his tongue.

'There's a church place around the corner,' said Leland, coming to sit nearby. 'They let you have one meal a day. Wholesome stuff.'

Kevin nodded. 'Sounds delightful. You here alone, then? Where's your brother?'

'He's near. Lives with his girlfriend.'

'What's back in Minnesota? Got any land?'

'No land. Nothing's back in Minnesota. Listen, you said you was lookin' for people. For what, exactly? Work?'

'Don't worry, Leland, your spot's guaranteed.'

'Can you take my brother on?'

'Sorry, no. This is good coffee. Leland, I'll explain after we've eaten.'

The weather had deteriorated overnight. They put on coats and walked the few blocks to an old warehouse building. There was a small queue of men which they joined. The phrase, *Soup Kitchen* came to Kevin's mind as he stood there with his collar up against the bitter wind. He could have imagined himself back in the Thirties but for the man in front with MP3 earphones in.

Once admitted they filed straight over to the kitchen serving hatches, Leland handing him a tray and plastic cutlery. Somebody was laughing in the kitchen, which surprised Kevin. When it was his turn to be served he saw that the joviality was coming from a large black chef.

'Honey, what hit you?' The question came from an equally large black woman who was in the line of servers, primed to slop something on his plate.

Kevin felt well enough to go with the running joke, and indicated Leland. 'Him.'

'Well, it seems you're still buddies. How would you like some of these here pork chops?'

'Good, ma'am, thank you.'

Two chops were placed on his plate. It was the mashed

potato and peas which were sloshed on and he had to shuffle forward towards the gravy jug. Leland overtook him and they picked out seats at wooden benches. Pitchers of water and plastic tumblers sat in the middle of each table.

'Will we get religion spouted at us?' asked Kevin.

'Sometimes there's that. Maybe not today. Good and warm in here, though.'

'Yes, very cosy.'

'That's Michelle you spoke to. She's a very nice lady. Her husband's the big chef, Devin.'

'Devin? That's like saying Kevin with a heavy cold.'

Leland laughed.

'I'll have to come here again,' said Kevin.

THREE

In Blackpool, private investigator, Jon Armstrong, had stayed in a B&B that seemed to have stepped back in time to the 1950s. All the furniture was antique; there was no television, of course, he had been warned by the buxom Landlady about bringing a woman back to his room, and it had cost him only about £10 in vouchers.

Still hungry after his bacon, eggs and something resembling a sausage, he left his Land Rover where it was and walked the streets, accosting youngsters with Leila's photograph. Just before lunchtime he got lucky, with a fervently positive ID and definite directions from a dreadlocked person of indistinguishable sex. He decided to buy a cheese and pickle sandwich and coke before heading off into the back streets to the address given to him. It started to rain, taking even more colour out of run down Blackpool, making him think he was playing a role in a Richard Attenborough or a John Mills movie.

He counted down the numbers on the correct street. Some

houses were occupied and some were vacant. Some were burnt out shells. The right one was occupied, but it shouldn't have been. It was clearly derelict. Obviously it had been turned into a kind of hippy flower-power squat. A man in a sheepskin coat was looking at him from the one downstairs window that wasn't boarded up. Jon hoped his information was wrong about Leila. He went up in search of a bell. It was an old bell-pull that had been pulled too far. The door opened and he was faced by two young men and a pit bull terrier. He was pleased to see the dog was on a lead.

'Sorry to bother you, lads. I'm looking for a girl called Leila.' He offered the photo up for their examination.

'Who's asking?' came from the lad holding the dog.

Jon noted there had been no immediate negative answer.

'A friend. Tell her it's Jon from London. Jon with the Aston Martin.' That didn't go down too well. He tried again. 'I know her brother, Musa. That'll identify me to her.'

'There's no one here by that name,' said the other youth. When Jon waved the photo, he said, 'Or anyone looking like that.'

Jon knew then that she was there. He weighed up his options. The dog looked the most docile pit bull he had ever seen in his life, but he didn't want to put it to the test. Right on cue, there came a shout from the top floor. He stepped back and looked up into the rain.

'Hey, Jon! It's Leila!'

'Leila, hi! Come down, they won't let me in!' He looked at

the men with the dog. 'You won't, will you?' They both shook their heads.

'I'm on my way down!'

The rain seemed to ease as Jon stood there looking at the two doormen. Then Leila jumped past the men as if they were her harmless kid brothers and was in his arms, being spun around. She was giddy with excitement. He put her down to look at her. Her hair was a mess but not dreadlocked. Her smiling face was as gorgeous as he remembered, though now more mature. What he had to deal with most about her was the multi-coloured thing she was wearing. It was an item of woollen clothing that went from her neck to her thighs, only describable to people familiar with the professor on British TV's *Time Team*. It was that bad.

She dragged him into the hall of the house, kissing the two men and a dog as they went.

'Through here,' she said. 'The kitchen; it's empty at the moment.' He was sat down on a grossly ornate wooden bench that must have come from a monastery. 'Do you want a cup of tea? How did you find me? What are you doing here? Do you want to have sex?' She cringed at the memory of the casual offer she had once made to him, and put her face in her hands. He laughed with her. 'What was I like back then? So immature.'

'Calm down, Leila. I've just come to see you.'

'Let's have a cup of tea. That'll calm me down.' She stood up to fill the old-style kettle at the sink. 'I don't see anyone from the old days. What a shock to have you here? Are you still with that girl in London? The one who found me coming out of your shower?'

'No, she didn't make it through.'

Leila lost her jollity. 'Oh, Jon, I'm so sorry.'

They didn't say anything more while she brewed up. She gave him his cup and led him out. 'We'll go up to my room. I share with a girl called Jo, but she's probably out shoplifting.'

They mounted the rickety stairs, all the way to the top floor. Leila's room was at the front. It was dark inside, sheets at the window, a lot of heavy dark wood furniture as if the room had been used for storage when they took it over. Leila was excited to have him sit beside her on her bed. They sipped their tea for a while.

'How's Musa?' he asked. 'You know, I'm the one who told him where you were. He finally tracked me down – a mercenary coming to my home and asking what had I got his little sister into. But he was really polite after I told him and thanked me and set off for the mall.'

'Musa's dead. Oh, nothing to do with the trouble. He was knocked down by a van about six months ago.'

'Oh, Leila. What about your other brother?'

'No idea.'

'Your mother?'

'Styal prison was one of the first places to go up.'

'So now you're here.'

She looked around her little room.

'I didn't mean that nastily,' he hurried to say. 'It must be... difficult.'

'It's not too bad. This place is run by oldies who've been squatting for years. It's all committees and votes. We have lots of fun.'

'Well, that's good.'

She bounced a little. 'So, why are you looking for me again?' When he decided to drink some tea first she knew she must wait for his explanation. She touched his knee. 'Remember when we first met? You took me to the Pleasure Beach.'

'Yeah. Shall we go again?'

'We can't, it's closed.'

'Bugger. Well, never mind, I suppose it is winter.'

'No, I mean, burned to the ground closed.'

'Ah.'

'It really is great to see you again.'

He was about to ask how she came to be living in a squat, when there came the sound of a herd of elephants charging up the stairs. He wondered whether he was about to be evicted unceremoniously. Instead of a gang entering the room, Leila's room mate burst in, dragging a gormless young man behind her, clearly excited about the possibility of some daytime sex. They both stopped dead on seeing Leila and her visitor.

'Jo, hi,' said Leila.

'I'm sorry,' said Jo, 'I didn't think you'd be up here.'

Jo was, what is described as, a big girl. Jon looked at her, and thought if she lost a few stone she was probably as pretty as Leila.

'This is an old friend of mine,' introduced Leila. 'Jon, this is Jo.'

Jon smiled and nodded.

'This is Seamus,' said Jo. 'Say hello, Seamus.'

'Hello,' said Seamus.

Leila stood up, prompting Jon to follow suit. 'We're just going out,' she said. 'Get out of your way.'

'You don't have to,' protested Jo, unconvincingly.

They all shuffled around each other, before Leila remembered that what she was wearing wasn't fit for public consumption, so they shuffled back again. 'I'll just put something better on.' She whipped off the multi-coloured *Time Team* sweater right in front of them and moved around in her bra looking for something to put on. The expression of Seamus's face suggested he was thinking he had come to the right place.

Leila settled on a tee-shirt and her coat and the shuffle resumed, with goodbyes offered all round. The doormen had vanished when they got downstairs and, as they left, Jon noticed that the front door didn't actually have any locks on it. They walked out into bright sunshine. As there wasn't a car, Leila took his hand and they strolled off in the direction of the sea front.

'Are you going to buy me lunch?' she asked.

'Don't I always?'

Andy Ding arrived in New Milford and, frankly, didn't think much of the place. After checking the information in his file, he asked a local man for directions to the street where Lee and Claudia lived. He drove up and down it a few times before setting out to find a coffee shop – he didn't want to just knock on their door, so would spend some time on stake-out duty, hoping to see them emerge.

The coffee shop he found seemed to be staffed by senior citizens. As he waited in line he went through his itinerary again: a male widower of upstanding character. The silver-haired barista who offered to take his order seemed a decent candidate. Perhaps he was retired from a position of authority, working in the shop because his pension had gone up in flames. But when the moment came, Andy couldn't form the question in his head. Instead, he ordered his favourite coffee and headed back to the car.

He returned to his target street and parked where he could see the entrance to Lee and Claudia's building. Out of habit, he moved across to sit on the passenger side, so that to a casual observer he would appear to be waiting for the driver to return. About half an hour in, Andy noticed something coming down the street that he had heard about but always thought was an urban legend. A bag lady, wearing a heavy, ragged, grey overcoat and fur boots, came by, pushing all her worldly possessions piled high in a shopping trolley. Now he came to think about it, Andy remembered such a sight as being part of the opening credits to an Eighties cop show. As the woman came parallel with the car, Andy tried to identify the contents of the trolley, but it was all too jumbled up. She was certainly missing the TV set balanced at a precarious angle. The old woman had a mass of grey hair and at first glance he thought her face was dirty. On closer inspection she was clearly of Native American extract, and very dignified at that. With his bonus in mind, Andy put the cold coffee he had been nursing into the cup holder and got out of the BMW – here was the mature woman in his file. He jogged over the road to engage her in conversation. Immediately it was heavy going, having to repeat himself and prevent her from walking off a couple of times. Finally she stopped believing he was crazier than she was and started to take in what he was saying. From then on she was putty in his hands, as soon as he instantly started to look after her. She wanted... she wanted, that was it, a hot roast beef sandwich and coffee. Andy nodded his agreement, thinking "one down, three to go". Only when she insisted on taking her possessions with her did he ever so slightly regret his rush of blood. All her junk was packed into the BMW before she placed herself haughtily in the passenger seat. Andy got behind the wheel and drove her away in search of a roast beef sandwich. Before they were off the block he realised that she reeked a little bit.

FOUR

Kevin went back alone the next day to the Christian soup kitchen, where his heavily bruised face was recognised by Michelle through the serving hatch. She served him macaroni cheese, which he consumed alongside his two new best friends, scraggly-bearded elderly men, who came to sit up close and personal to him. Their conversation was harmless nonsense, concerning their histories and current troubles, but it was all put across quite aggressively because they wanted him to either understand or sympathise with them. Kevin was reminded of an old Billy Connolly joke about a tramp on a bus making him have one of his sweets, despite several polite refusals. After finally taking a sweet, indicating that it was lovely, the tramp informed him, "that's been up my bum". Kevin laughed out loud and his two friends gaped at him.

He lingered around after his meal. Two officials from the shelter tried to talk to him but he fobbed them off. He watched Michelle and her husband, Devin, cleaning down after service, then sought them out in a back alleyway where they were smoking cigarettes. Kevin had fun over the introductions of a Devin to a Kevin, then he lit up his own smoke and gave them the proposal in his best salesman spiel.

After Kevin had left them to think it over, saying he would return the following day for their answer, they sat there quietly discussing it all. The couple were originally from Brooklyn, Illinois. They had been forced into the big city when their farm, which their family had owned since the 1870s, went bust during the trouble. They were an indomitably happy couple, who loved everything to do with food and cooking as well as their current position. But what the Englishman had just said to them created new and vast possibilities.

Leila took Jon to see where the tower used to be. Even though he was looking at vacant space it was somehow eerie. Then they took a ride in a horse-drawn carriage, something he had deliberately given a wide berth to the last time he was in Blackpool. It was a pleasant surprise, the sun just strong enough to keep the chill off, and Leila snuggled into him as if they were boyfriend and girlfriend.

'There's our bus shelter,' she suddenly cried out, pointing, 'where we first met. Isn't it romantic that it's still there? There aren't any buses running any more, but at least the shelter's still up.'

'I thought you were a right hooligan that day, in your hoodie. Then you threw it off your head and smiled at me. What was it you were listening to on your iPod? Paul Weller? How bizarre.'

During the length of the carriage ride along the prom,

Leila heard the reason for Jon looking for her again. The news spoilt her appetite in the pizza place they picked out. Then they walked back to the house squat, hand in hand.

'Let me find you a hotel,' he offered. 'I'm in a great B&B, myself.'

'No, Jon, I live here.'

He glanced down at his feet, more guilty than ever for tracking her down. 'I suppose I'll see you tomorrow, then. Let you sleep on it.'

'No, come in. I want you to meet Bernie and Robert. They run the place.'

He grinned. 'You know, two years ago I avoided meeting your foster parents.'

'God, they're nothing like those two. They'll like you, I'm sure of it.'

She dragged him into the house and left him sitting in the front room while she went in search of the leaders of the group. Jon looked about him in the gloomy, very cluttered room, with dirty net curtains and masses of brown furniture. It reminded him of one of those TV documentaries on hoarders. There was a high-back smoking chair that his eyes came to rest on, mainly because there seemed to be a grey corpse sitting in it. But then the hands moved to turn the page of a book and the eyes, surrounded by wild grey hair and beard, turned to look at him. The man resembled Sean Connery in *The Rock*, before the barber visited him in the hotel.

'Oh, hello,' said Jon. 'I didn't see you there at first.'

The man placed a bookmark in his book and set it down, then slowly crossed his legs. 'Good afternoon,' he said. 'You're the one who's come for Leila.'

Jon nodded. 'That's one way of putting it.'

'May I tell you something? I'm quite taken with our Leila. She's an extraordinary young lady – all she's been through, and I don't mean since the troubles, or even to what happened down in Berkshire, but life before, when she was in care. And still she's grown up to be a delightful person. She's still a bit feisty, not shy about throwing a punch or two, but we all love her to bits here.'

'I can understand that. You know what happened in Berkshire, then? Down in the mall?'

'Yes, my friend, I do. Oh, I'm sorry. I'm Charlie. Charlie Barnes.'

Jon rushed to his feet to offer a handshake. 'Jon Armstrong. Good to meet you, Mr Barnes.'

'Please, call me Charlie. Good to make your acquaintance too, Jon.'

'Are you from Blackpool, Charlie?

'Am I from Blackpool? No, I'm from Warrington, technically. Let me ask you, what were those fake zombies supposed to be doing at that shopping centre? They were drawn towards something familiar. Isn't that what the famous film had them doing? I suppose I gravitated towards somewhere I associated with happy family memories, here by the seaside. It was bad here, but there was nothing left of Warrington.'

'I'm sorry to hear that, Charlie.'

Leila skipped into the room. Her face broke into a wonderful smile on seeing Charlie Barnes and she leant over to hug him. 'I see you two are getting along. Can I steal him away, Charlie?'

Charlie raised a hand. 'He's all yours, Leila. We were just shooting the breeze.'

Jon allowed himself to be led out, nodding to Charlie as he went.

Andy's bag lady was called Ruth Rigsby and she was a very small part Iroquois Indian. That's what she told him anyway, without him even asking. She was installed in a modest hotel, but only after he had negotiated special rates with the management because, a) they knew her and, b) they knew her.

Andy returned to Lee and Claudia's stakeout, unfazed by the possibility of hours of just sitting there. But then, because he was on a roll, he decided to return to the senior citizen's coffee shop, where he sought out an interview with the grey-haired gentleman who had served him earlier. His business proposal received a horrified reaction and a hurried moving away. Luckily, the barista's colleague happened to be earwigging nearby and stepped in when Andy was left alone, wondering if the cops were about to be called.

'I'd like to hear you out,' said the man, equally grey-haired, aged about sixty. 'My name's Phil Bennington.'

Andy assessed the tall, distinguished man in front of him. The apron, the towel and the slight sheen of sweat on his high, tanned forehead didn't quite sit right – here was a man whose pension had indeed gone up in flames and left him wondering what to do.

'Mr Bennington, I'd be glad to tell you.'

After his shift, Phil Bennington walked to the rooms he rented in a large house on Church street. He lived in one of the rooms, slept in the other, and his lifetime possessions were boxed in the third. He threw his apron and waistcoat onto the couch and went to fill the kettle. As he stood at the sink, he looked over his shoulder towards the "ornamental" TV set. Sitting atop that was the one photo on show, that of his late wife, Evelyn.

'What do you think?' he asked the photograph.

He clicked the kettle on and spooned the last of his instant coffee into a mug. He had a good scratch at his forehead – he was sluggish, nervous, in three minds. Andy had stunned him with the enormity of the proposal on offer.

'I know what you'd do,' he said to his wife. 'Grab it with both hands.' He reached for milk from the fridge. 'What to do? What to do?' The kettle boiled, he made his coffee, then sat down by the window to watch the world go by. Not much world went by during the next hour that he was sitting there.

The next day, Andy drove his BMW out of New Milford the way he had come in. He stopped at the same garage and was pleased to find the surly young Swede on duty again. The Swede enquired if there was a problem with the puncture repair. When Andy assured him that everything was fine, and the Swede just stared at him, wiping his hands on a rag, Andy had to come straight to the point. As he listened, the Swede stared even harder.

As Andy's BMW drove away, a door to the apartment above the garage opened, and a cute, blonde girl came down the stairs at the side of the building.

'Kurt, is anything wrong?' she asked.

'Nah,' answered Kurt, without bothering to move his lips.

The blonde was called Brook, Kurt's seventeen-year-old girlfriend. Brook had grown up in a place called Bettendorf in Iowa, on the banks of the Mississippi, where her father ran a garage. From an early age she had loved motor racing, especially Formula One, and her favourite driver had been the Finn, Kimi Raikonnen: a supremely talented and interesting man, but one who seemed to hardly ever say a word to anyone in public. That was what appealed to Brook most when Kurt had shown up to work for her father six months previously; he was very handsome, Scandinavian and, basically, monosyllabic.

Their immediate, intense relationship had caused ructions in the household, a fight even, with her two older brothers (which Kurt had nearly won with his well-hidden violent temper) and eventually came their flight to Connecticut and this garage, owned by associates of Kurt's relatives.

Brook felt she loved Kurt. Her estrangement from her family had come surprisingly easily, especially with her mother already deceased. She only wanted to care for Kurt. As he seemed more distant than usual, she held him from behind, worried for him.

'Man offered me a job,' said Kurt, indicating the direction in which Andy's car had gone.

'A job? Where?'

Kurt turned in her embrace and they kissed leisurely.

'Texas,' he said. 'I think he might be a little crazy.'

Thirty-six hours passed before Lee and Claudia showed themselves to Andy Ding. He was staying in the same cheap hotel as Ruth Rigsby, around the corner, and walked with his coffee and doughnut breakfast to where he had left the BMW the previous day. Lee and Claudia wheeled bicycles out of their building and rode off together, happy and laughing. Andy was puzzled by Lee's white flared trousers below his heavy coat. He started his engine and slowly followed them along the street.

They led him to the building on Railway street. The mixed group of people waiting for Lee unnerved Andy slightly, but when Lee unlocked the building and all the people cheerily filed in, he felt emboldened. Lee and Claudia were kissing –

she was clearly about to carry on to her own destination. Andy took his chance, parked the BMW and approached the couple.

'Lee?' he called out.

Lee and Claudia paused in their romantic clinch, before Lee happily gestured at Claudia as if to say, "there you go, a new student, we're not bankrupt".

'Hello there,' answered Lee. 'Are you looking to join my club?'

Not one for easy banter, Andy managed to answer, 'I may be.'

'Well, you're welcome to watch the lesson. It's an hour long. Then we can have a chat.'

'Could we talk first?'

Claudia made to leave, pointing her bike in a different direction before kissing Lee. 'Off to work. I'll see you later, baby.'

'I'd like to talk to you as well, Claudia,' said Andy.

That stopped her dead and she glared at the man. 'Who the hell are you?' she asked.

He gave them his name. 'I've been detailed to talk to you about a six month confinement, hiding away from a zombie apocalypse.'

Claudia tried to approach Andy, as if to tackle him, maybe slap his face, but was hindered by the bicycle between her legs. 'We don't want to talk about that. We're trying to forget all that.'

'Who are you?' asked Lee. 'A reporter?'

'No, I'm not a reporter. If this is an inconvenient time, I could meet you later today.'

'Never mind that,' said Lee, beginning to get annoyed. 'Why do you want to drag all that up again? We're just trying to get on with our lives here.'

'Yes,' said Claudia. 'Why don't you just fuck off?'

Andy said, 'I understand this is a delicate matter. It really would be in your interest...'

Claudia had managed to disentangle herself from her bike and put in a slap to the left side of Andy's face. He took it remarkably well with only a slow blink of the eyes.

'I have to pass on the message,' said Andy. 'It would be to your advantage to hear me out. Then I'll never bother you again.'

Claudia looked like she wanted to slap Andy's other cheek. Lee held her around the waist, and the appearance in the doorway of one of Lee's students, in his dobok and green belt, interrupted the confrontation. It was the large man whose discomfort Claudia found amusing whenever he was made to run around the room.

'We're ready when you are, chief,' said the big student, looking quizzically at Andy. 'Get the pain over with, shall we?'

Lee broke off from looking at Andy. 'Of course, mate. Right with you.' He slapped the student on the back, before turning to Andy again. 'Come back in an hour.'

'No, Lee,' protested Claudia. 'I should be here too.'

'Come out of the bakery, then. Make some excuse. I want

this over with. We'll hear him out and he can go on his way.'

Andy gestured his acceptance, then nodded courteously at a furious Claudia, and backed away.

Lee embraced Claudia, kissing her forehead. 'He probably is from the press. Pop back in an hour, yeah. We'll tell him where to go if we don't like what he's saying.'

'Can I hit him again?'

'Best not. When a man doesn't seem to mind being slapped, it's probably wise not to slap him.'

Lee worked his students manically over the next hour, almost taking the big student to the brink of collapse. Everyone was red-faced and blowing as they filed out, Lee bidding them goodbye. He was shattered himself, ready for his shower when he got home. He went to the building's bathroom, where he drank some water and splashed his raging hot face. As he looked at himself in the mirror he allowed himself to think about those times with Claudia, and Leila, in Berkshire. The first part of it had been interesting, wonderful even. To leave his relationship with that girl in Liverpool and set off on the strangest adventure of his life. To bond straight off with the crazy kid, Leila, naturally slipping into a relationship with her, however bizarre the circumstances. There was the friendship with the American man, Madesio, from New York, with the big family. What became of him? Or of Cathy, from Buffalo, who took her place in the mall to get over her split from her fiancé.

Lee thought of Leila again, of her troubled personality and

nubile body, sharing intimacy with him through the changing atmosphere over the months, finally giving him to Claudia because "you two make a lovely couple", even taking offence when Claudia suggested they leave well alone until the experiment came to an end. Funny girl, that Leila, he chuckled to his reflection, wondering what had become of her. He hoped she was all right.

He went back into his dojang. Claudia was entering with Andy Ding in tow. It didn't look like there had been any fresh violence, but he hurried over.

'Take your shoes off, please,' Lee said to Andy.

Andy complied immediately without complaint, suggesting a familiarisation himself with martial arts. With the room being bare of furniture, Lee gestured for them to sit on the floor. Again, no problem to Andy. They sat down, Claudia close to Lee, she being the only one to be slightly embarrassed with the location of the meeting. Lee performed some necessary warm-down stretches once in position.

'Thank you for this,' said Andy. 'Shall I start?'

'The sooner you start,' said Claudia, 'the sooner you go away.'

'That's very true, miss. Right, I'm not here to talk about what happened in England. I'm here to invite you to take part in the new experiment that starts, in Texas I believe, next month.'

Lee continued his warm-down, rubbing his calves. Claudia's face was fixed like stone.

'Payment this time will not be money. This time it will be land. Several hundred acres per person from the estate of the late Mr Michael Hester in the United States.'

Claudia winced at the mention of Hester's name – memories flooded back to her of how they had become virtual prisoners towards the end of the stay in Berkshire. Memories of the madness of Hester and his people as they realised his plans were not going to pan out. She looked at Lee. Without him, right then she could have been living in Hester's commune in upstate New York.

'Now, I know something of what happened last time,' said Andy. 'But there's no reason to see anything bad in this new proposition. It's just a way to distribute the spare land. Everyone is to gather at the stepping off point in Chicago in fourteen days time.'

'Who's everyone?' asked Lee.

'I have a young Swedish man called Kurt Gustafson, and two people from New Milford, Phil Bennington and Ruth Rigsby. I don't know who else has been signed up elsewhere.'

Claudia had turned to combing her hair with her fingers. She looked to Lee again. 'Is he still here?'

'Still here, babe. He wants us to do it all again.'

'Why us?'

'Why us?' Lee asked Andy. Andy shrugged. 'He doesn't know.'

'I want to hit him again, Lee.'

'What did I tell you about that?'

They sat in silence on the floor for a moment.

'What's in Texas?' Lee asked Andy.

'I don't know what's in Texas.'

'How many people?'

'Fourteen or fifteen, I think.'

'Anybody from the shopping mall?'

'I've no idea.'

'Who's behind this? Who's your boss?'

'The man I'm answerable to in Chicago is called Frankie King.'

Claudia's head shot up. 'Frankie King?!'

Andy asked, deadpan, 'Would you like to slap him?'

Frankie King had been one of the organisers for Michael Hester's project.

Lee smiled. 'I quite liked the guy.'

'I'm sure he'll have all the answers for you,' said Andy.

'I said I liked him, not that I had any intention of ever seeing him again.'

'As you wish. I've said my piece.' Andy took out a pen and a sheet of paper and wrote down a phone number. 'I leave for Chicago in four days.'

Lee took the paper. He made sure to stand up at the same time as Andy. Andy politely acknowledged Claudia again.

'Whatever,' she said to him.

They watched Andy leave the dojang. Lee squatted in front of Claudia. She rested her hands on his knees.

'Are you all right?' he asked.

'Not sure. That wasn't something I wanted to hear.'

'Yeah, bit of a shock.'

She cried a little. He comforted her.

'Get up off that cold floor,' he told her. 'Let's go home.'

She let him pull her to her feet. She laughed involuntarily. 'Home? A tiny apartment in New Milford?'

He held her. 'I thought you liked New Milford?'

'I do. I just wish I could go home to my mum and dad in York. But that's not to be.'

'He's upset you. I'm sorry.'

'He has upset me. Started me thinking about the future, though. Where will we call home, Lee? Here?' She paused. 'You're not thinking of listening to that man, are you?'

'No, of course not.'

'Because, even if it's a straightforward game this time, it's still crazy. What do we need to do that nonsense again for?'

GB Hope

FIVE

'What do you think to Daniel Craig playing me in the movie of this thing?'

'But Daniel Craig's a good-looking bloke.'

Frankie King laughed, and Carly Radcliffe smirked as she went to do her make-up in the bathroom mirror. Frankie was reclined on his bed in his Chicago hotel suite. He had the whole floor to himself, not because his employer had paid for it, just that no one else could afford to stay there. He was still thrilled to be in Chicago, the home to his childhood fascination with mobsters and Al Capone and John Dillinger, and on his stomach lay a handgun that he continually fondled, aimed at the walls and weighed in his hand. He loved the weapon which had been given to him by one of his staff. He was unconcerned that it didn't have any bullets in it, or even that it was a Colt single action revolver from the 1870's – he was packing iron in Chicago!

And there was a gangster's moll in the bathroom. Actually, Carly Radcliffe was his assistant, and his new lover as of three weeks ago. She was one of those Australians who had come north since the troubles of 2016, not to work in a London pub, but to make her fortune amid the chaos and rebuilding efforts. She was a spiky, short-bobbed redhead, who did a lot of shouting for him as they tried to put all the groundwork in place for the new project.

He had tried to resist getting involved again in something so mental. Finding the people for the shopping mall had been his craziest job ever and, after the way that had ended, it was the last thing in his mind to go and do it again. But then they offered him an exciting stretch of real estate in New Hampshire (not somewhere he was familiar with) and if the world ever got back to normal then he would be a wealthy man.

'I've decided to have sushi,' called Carly.

'Good for you. Make sure to let me know how it was.'

'Are you against that idea? What do you fancy?'

'Cooked food.'

Carly came back into the bedroom to slip into her dress. She still seemed to be a while off being ready to go down to dinner, so Frankie weighed the gun in his other hand and thought some more about the job – why was his bonus conditional on signing up three of those people who made it out of the mall? On three of the people who left Michael Hester dead on the car-park, three people he remembered from the private investigator reports and from meeting them in that London hotel? Lee, Claudia and Leila. He was excited to be meeting them again in the morning.

'You know,' said Carly, indicating the Colt, 'You're not supposed to take that out unless you intend to use it.'

'I bet you say that to all the boys.'

It was down to Carly to meet the cars in the hotel portico. Leland from Minnesota was first to arrive. He apparently cleaned up well – shaven, new clothes, refreshed, and he had taken Kevin Reed's advice not to take his gun along with him. He would be frisked at some stage anyway. He shook Carly's hand and let her lead him into the foyer.

'Is there anything you need?' Carly asked him.

'No, I'm good, thank you.'

'Let's get you checked in. There'll be a medical within the hour. If you want to see a dentist, we have one on standby.'

Leland seemed to wonder about that, perhaps thinking he might as well take advantage of the offer.

'Mr King will come to see you soon.'

Carly was hyper, with four months of planning coming to a head that day. She had the cars coming in at ten minute intervals and was back outside in time for Charlie Barnes. The man from the Blackpool squat was at least clean, but he had chosen not to visit a barber and carried his silver hair pulled back into a ponytail – he looked less like Sean Connery in *The Rock* and more like some kind of guru. He was clearly nervous, and when Carly asked if he needed anything, he responded with a list which included malt whisky, a cheese and pickle sandwich and some reiki massage. She booked him in at reception before handing him over to a helpful member of the hotel staff who would procure those things. Carly decided not to ask the others if they had any extraordinary requirements.

Phil Bennington, from New Milford, was next to arrive. Carly puzzled over why the famous Leila had not followed on from Charlie, then welcomed Phil with a broad smile. 'Let's get you checked in, Phil. You'll have a medical within the hour. Do you need a dentist?' He declined. 'Walk this way. I like that jacket.'

He was in a navy-blue Timberland coat, with heavy boots and a NY Mets baseball cap. He was geared up for a mission. The pockets of his desert camo' trousers carried a lock-knife, his blood pressure tablets, nasal spray, antibiotics, three types of mints and some of those bourbon biscuits.

A different member of the hotel staff took Phil away to his room.

Carly wandered back outside. Here was Leila! She was just stepping from a Mercedes. Frankie King had talked about a cute wildcat of a girl – this was a sexy teenage woman with long legs in dark jeans, a thick sweater with hood up and a large rucksack on her back, which would have to be checked for contraband.

'You must be Leila. I'm Carly.' Leila nodded but didn't return Carly's smile. 'You're an old hand at this, I believe.' Leila's po-face checked Carly's enthusiasm. 'Sorry, I realise it's a big decision to enter into something like this again.'

'Is Charlie here? I'd like to see him.'

'He's here. But I think he might be having his medical about now. You'll meet everybody very soon. Come along, we'll check you in. Do you need to see a dentist?'

'What?'

'Oh, never mind. Are you hungry?'

'A bit.'

Leila allowed herself to be guided into the hotel with all the enthusiasm of a new inmate to a 19th century workhouse. 'What did you say your name was?'

'It's Carly.'

'Carly, what are the other people like? Jon Armstrong is a sweetheart, but he couldn't tell me.'

Carly could see how much this point meant to Leila. 'A very mixed group. They're mostly Americans, one young Swedish man – a bit moody, maybe you two will hit it off!' She laughed. This was tough. 'Let me think, we have a doctor from Chicago, and a teenage man from Minnesota. Charlie Barnes you know, of course…'

'Charlie!'

Leila dashed across the foyer to where Charlie Barnes had appeared, wandering without a care in the world, one hand carrying a glass of whisky, the other a sandwich. Trailing behind came the harassed member of staff detailed to him.

'Hello, darling,' said Charlie, letting Leila embrace him. 'You got here safely, then?'

'Thank God you're here, Charlie.'

'We'll be all right, kid. Would you like a sandwich? I've got a huge platter through there.'

'I'd love a sandwich.'

Ignoring Carly, who was seeing her schedule being torn up, they walked off. Carly waved frantically for the hotel worker to stay with them.

'Fucking poms,' muttered Carly, as she headed back outside.

She found Devin and Michelle, clearly wondering why they had not been met. Was it because they were black?

'Michelle, Devin, welcome!'

When he had set up the event in Berkshire, Frankie King had been proud of the scale model of the shopping mall he'd had made up, and which had been placed in the conference room in London, where the people initially gathered. It had been a pointless expense but, hell, the whole thing had been one great big money pit. Now he stood in the conference room in the Chicago hotel admiring a new model – one that would offer no clothes shopping, no food outlets, no sports games to play or bicycles to ride, not even electricity. He grinned, thinking how harsh it was going to be, and wondering if any of them would quit straight off the bat.

Frankie headed to the front of house to see how Carly was getting along. He found her with most of the contestants, all chatting to each other a few hours before they were supposed to meet – Charlie and Leila apparently drinking hard liquor. Leland and Kurt were deep in conversation, Devin and Michelle had gotten sandwiches from somewhere. Dr Holloway stood talking to a small, neatly dressed woman who he didn't recognise. Then he realised the woman was Ruth Rigsby from New Milford. After he had found out that she was a homeless bag lady he had almost vetoed her presence. He was pleased he hadn't now. He caught Carly's eye and she shrugged with embarrassment at the lack of order. He just shook his head and grinned at her.

Phil Bennington joined the gathering, buttoning his shirt following his medical. He accepted a sandwich from Michelle and introduced himself.

Frankie stood with his arms crossed, satisfied that everything was working out anyway. To his left he saw more arrivals. Private Investigators: Jon Armstrong, Kevin Reed and Andy Ding, having completed their assignments, were in for the six month confinement themselves. They needed the new start that free land would give them as much as anyone. Frankie watched an astonished Leila jump into Jon's arms, wrapping her legs around his waist. He had clearly kept his inclusion a secret to her and she was telling him off. He made her get down. Her perfect teeth flashed into a fabulous smile as she handed him a glass of whisky. Jon accepted it and clinked glasses with Charlie.

Kevin was welcomed by Leland and Dr Holloway, who checked out his healing face. When Devin realised Kevin was amongst them he gave up a theatrical high five, while Michelle offered the sandwich platter.

Frankie went across to welcome Andy Ding, who seemed to be a bit lost because Lee and Claudia were yet to arrive, and Phil and Kurt were not looking to bond with him. Kurt, especially, came across as somewhat of a loner.

'Ready for this, Mr Ding?' asked Frankie.

'I think so, Mr King. Are you satisfied with the mix?'

Frankie appraised the group. 'A fantastic selection of people. We're just missing your other two from New Milford.'

'They just walked in.'

Frankie spun around. Lee and Claudia stood there holding hands, agog at the scene that faced them. They were both in heavy leather coats that went to their knees. She had on a cream baseball cap and he wore a Manchester City beanie hat. Each carried a rucksack - they were clearly going in ready this time. Frankie looked for Leila to gauge her reaction, and found her face just as she spotted her old mall-mates. She tried to keep her expression impassive, but there was a biting of her lower lip and clear emotion in the eyes.

SIX

After all the initial meetings in the foyer and general eyeing-up of their fellow internees, a number of factions developed: those satisfied with Michelle's sandwiches, and those keen to take advantage of Carly's urgings to sample the hotel's many food options; those with questions aplenty, and those just going with the flow. Kurt was the poster child for the last point. He seemed to exist in a permanent state of tranquillity, seeking neither food nor conversation. If he had been less photogenic, then the other people there may have been wary of him to the point of hostility.

Those people with the questions, but not the appetite, were first to have an audience with Frankie King. He told them they were headed for Texas, just as he had identified Berkshire first time round. They would be getting to the location by helicopter, then train. They shouldn't expect luxury. He took them through to the conference room for them to see his model.

'Well, my Lord,' said Phil Bennington. 'Is that what I think it is? It's a cavalry fort.'

'I had one of those as a child at home in Birmingham,' said Kevin Reed, genuinely excited. 'With little blue cavalry troopers.'

Devin and Michelle went up close to the model. It was made of dark wood, with overhanging blockhouse towers above the main entrance and at four of the six corners. A railway track ran right the way through the fort, exiting at the back to run over a bridge with a river underneath. Inside the compound stood one long barracks against a wall and several free-standing buildings.

As if by magic, Frankie wielded a pointer and put it to good use. 'Bunkhouse here, the long building. Cook-house, stores. Bathhouse/washhouse, call it what you want. Stables without horses. Latrines. Office. Jail. Another building, not sure what that one is. There's the well, for all your water.'

Michelle gave him her best "what you talkin' 'bout" expression. 'No running water, Mr King?'

'No, Michelle. Apparently, somewhere on a wall, there's a calendar that reads, June 1876.'

Kevin said, 'So no electricity? Basically then, glorified camping for six months. Jesus Christ!'

Frankie retired a little to let the shock sink in. Kevin's eyes followed him to the side wall, where a buffet was laid out. Frankie picked up a piece of fruit and offered it to Kevin. 'Have a banana.'

Those four drifted away, breaking the news to incoming Andy, Kurt, Charlie Barnes and Ruth Rigsby. The next wave took in the fort. Frankie waggled his pointer, coughed, and went through his presentation again.

Doc Holloway, Leland and Jon decided to eat in one of the hotel's bars, oblivious to what everyone else was finding out in the conference room. Lee, Claudia and Leila were nearby, drinking coffee. Leila had made the move towards them in the foyer, kissing cheeks (no air kissing), joking "What are we doing? We must be fucking mad!" Lee had stumbled over his greeting, delighted to see her alive and well, trying not to tell her she looked fabulous in front of Claudia. Here was his lover from the shopping mall who had passed him on to Claudia because she didn't want a boyfriend back in the real world. Here was the girl who was in Michael Hester's grasp at the end of the madness, up on the roof of the dome above the building, with Lee having to kill two men to get up there to try to save her. In the end, her brother Musa had saved the day with his execution of the crazed billionaire.

Leila and Claudia asked the same questions simultaneously: where have you been living? Leila talked of the people in the Blackpool squat. Claudia described their New Milford lives.

'Jon's going with us,' said Leila. 'He's the one who picked me up in 2016, and he found me again.'

'Strange, isn't it?' said Lee. 'Only the three of us included. We'll have to ask about the others.'

'Maybe they refused,' said Leila. 'Maybe they're dead. I lost Musa.'

Claudia took Leila's hand in sympathy.

Kevin wandered in, heading to the boys' table. 'It's a fucking Wild West fort,' he blurted out.

'You're kidding,' said the Doc.

'No, man. Wooden walls, no electricity. Who do we sue?'

Lee and the girls digested the news.

'God,' said Lee. 'A completely different set-up. What do we

think of that?'

'Peace and quiet,' answered Claudia. 'Might need some more batteries for the iPod.' She smiled at Leila. 'We've brought everything but the kitchen sink. I've got a Kindle. You can borrow it.'

Leila sipped her coffee. 'Why do you think this is happening?'

'No idea,' said Lee. 'We'll have to question Frankie King.'

'Now,' said Claudia. 'Let's have a go at him now.'

The three of them took directions from Kevin and went through to the conference room, to look at the fort. Frankie had served himself a coffee. He stepped towards them, still proud of his model. He shook hands with Lee.

'The originals,' said Frankie, smiling. 'Reformed for one more gig.'

'Yes,' said Claudia, firmly. 'But why us?'

'Why not? No, seriously, you three were identified to me when I was engaged again. Perhaps an initial search failed to show up any of the other... any of the others.'

'But why?' she persisted. 'Why are we doing it again?'

'I don't know, Claudia. But I don't think there's anything sinister behind it. Bizarre, yes. Sinister, no.'

Leila needed to visit the Ladies room, so Claudia went with her. Frankie relaxed when he was only in Lee's company.

'I don't suppose there's any point me asking you who's behind this adventure,' Lee asked. Frankie shook his head. 'So, it's a zombie thing again?'

'Yes. If you meet the really sneaky one that jumps at you, that was my idea. I'm proud of that.'

'Oh, right. I'll remember that. Have all the others been

warned not to mess with the robotic zombies?'

'Everyone knows what they're going into as far as the robots are concerned. Are you going to talk to the others about what happened in the mall?'

'We've not decided yet. If it is all sweetness and light this time, maybe we won't have to.'

'No, maybe not.'

'Did you consider going along?'

'No, now you mention it. Lee, I wish you a safe trip.'

'Thanks, Frankie.'

They shook hands again.

'So, fellas,' said Kevin to his group, sitting in the hotel bar. 'What do we think of the people we're going to be locked away with for six months?'

'Perhaps it's too early to tell,' suggested the Doc. 'Maybe we should wait until people's personalities come through over the coming days.'

Kevin considered that point of view, then completely disregarded it. 'What about that Claudia? Now, she's a hottie. Not forgetting what's-her-name, Leila. Well done there, Jon, by the way.'

Jon pretended to accept the praise.

'But apart from those two we're a little light on totty. Too many blokes. Jon, where did you find that old geezer, Charlie? Him, Phil and the Native American woman are a bit old for this game. And what about her? Ruth Rigsby. Rigsby? That's not a very Red Indian name, if you ask me.'

SEVEN

They left Chicago in a fleet of helicopters. Only Andy Ding assessed the position of the sun and announced to his group that they were heading west.

They came in over a small town and set down in the dusty wasteland of an industrial estate and railway goods yard. Like tour guides, Frankie and Carly gathered everyone to them and marched them away towards a nondescript warehouse building. They were all glad to get in out of the sun and dust. A team of two men and two women stood waiting for them, with beverages set out and bathroom facilities available.

Everyone took the opportunity to relax, knowing they would be thrown in at the deep end soon enough, and it was interesting to note that people who hadn't really got to meet in the hotel were sitting there in conversation.

They were then split into two groups according to sex, and taken into adjoining rooms to be frisked and have their bags checked for things such as weapons or drugs. Claudia looked at Leila, Michelle and Ruth, and realised she would be short on female friendship for the foreseeable future. As she was patted down by a woman who had introduced herself as Carmel, she said to Leila, 'Looks like we'll have to do without crack cocaine for six months.'

Leila smiled. She was handed back her rucksack by the other woman, Jessica.

Carmel asked, 'Ladies, are you ready to choose your costumes?'

'Costumes?' asked Michelle for all of them.

'This way please,' said Jessica.

They went further into the warehouse to a room which resembled a theatre props department, with metal cages piled with all kinds of tat, rows and rows of heavily-laden clothes racks and a long counter. The four women descended joyously on the old-fashioned dresses, pants, bloomers and little hats. There were corsets and knickerbockers, frilly blouses and high leather boots.

'You know you'll be living in a fort,' called Carmel. 'So you'll dress in the Old West fashion. You have two choices. You can dress as ladies or as cowgirls. Your regular clothes will go as well, don't worry, this is just for the journey.'

'Oh, wow,' said Claudia.

She and Leila pretended to fight over a green taffeta dress. Jessica waited at Claudia's elbow.

'Claudia, for you, can I make a suggestion?'

'Okay, Jessica, go ahead.'

Next door, the boys were universally thrilled, already in cowboy hats and black, tasselled waistcoats. Kurt was earnestly considering a pair of leather chaps, and Leland was choosing his boots. The two men in charge of them were called Zac and Barney. They tried to retain some semblance of order.

'Guys!' called Barney. 'Listen up, will ya, we've only got an hour. You're going back to the Wild West. Decide on your look. Keep it practical. Six months, remember. Heavy tops, jeans. If you didn't bring a big coat, check out the leathers and sheepskins.'

Surprisingly, the girls made it out first to the final stage of the fitting-out process, through to an outdoors area with a view over a dusty compound. Leila had gone for the cowgirl look, in jeans and pale shirt with a tan cowboy hat. Michelle was in a bright red taffeta skirt and white blouse. Ruth was very conservatively dressed in a dark wool frock coat over brown ankle length skirt, looking very much like a poor farmer's wife. Claudia was reliably informed by Jessica that she looked like Claudia Cardinale in *Once Upon A Time In The West*, even to the sexy little hat she had on.

Claudia looked out into the dusty haze, and then in front of her to several trestle tables, on which sat a variety of weapons from that bygone age. 'Guns?' she said to Jessica.

'Authentic props,' answered Jessica. 'For when the men come through. Some will have chosen to look like Billy The Kid, so they'll need the holster.'

The boys came out as a noisy rabble. Jon, Kevin and Andy led the way, looking like regular cowboys. It was Leland who had gone for the gunslinger look, all in black. Lee was next out, in full navy-blue cavalry outfit, complete with yellow stripe down each leg, riding boots and peaked forage cap. Claudia almost collapsed in hysterics. He let her get it out of her system before they embraced and he made fun of her outfit too.

'I'm supposed to be Claudia Cardinale,' she told him, in all seriousness.

'What do you think?' he asked, checking his jacket buttons.

'You've forgot your spurs.'

Kurt came through, seemingly embarrassed in his cowboy outfit. Devin arrived and went straight to heap praise upon Michelle's appearance. Then Charlie and Phil appeared together, both in suits and waistcoats of the time, with derby hats in place. The Doc was last out into the sunshine. The others had made him dress like Doc Holliday, with a fancy waistcoat and necktie, and he had gone along with it in good grace.

'The Doc gets the prize,' called Kevin, laughing. 'But I'm not sure about you, Andy. Shouldn't you be dressed like...' He aborted the Chinaman joke and turned his attention to the others. 'Why, you all look brilliant, ladies. Ruth, shouldn't you be...' He left the Red Indian squaw gag also hanging. He turned to Devin and Michelle. They cheerfully warned him away from any slave jibe.

Leland moved near to Leila. 'You look great,' he told her.

'Thank you. Are you supposed to be Billy the Kid?'

'No fear. I'm the Sundance Kid.'

'Oh, of course you are.' As she talked, she was checking out Jon's appearance, and that of Lee. 'Robert Redford, yeah?'

'That's right. I know I don't look like him, but I liked that film.'

'Apparently, I'm supposed to be Ann Margret in *The Train Robbers*. No, I haven't a clue what that means, either.'

Zac and Barney had come outside and positioned themselves behind the trestle tables, waiting for order. There then followed the full gamut of reaction as everybody realised there were to be firearms with them on the adventure. Kevin was loudly delighted, hugging Leland, the man who had attempted to rob him at gunpoint in Chicago. Jon was intrigued, the Doc nervously keen, Kurt showing an interest. Claudia just turned away, looking at an equally concerned Lee. Michelle was most vocal in her disapproval, with Devin on his wife's side.

'Count me out,' said Phil.

Charlie was of the same mind. 'Yes, I'm not comfortable with doing that.'

'That's okay, gentlemen,' said Zac. 'It's entirely your choice. Those who want to carry a firearm, please pay attention.'

He picked up the quintessential cowboy gun, exactly like the one Frankie had been playing with in his hotel suite. At the same time, Barney held up a Winchester rifle, unmistakable from any cowboy film. They then launched into a tutorial on how to handle the weapons safely, how to load, what kind of ammunition they held, then they allowed the cowboys to fire off their weapons into the wasteland in front of them.

Those unsure of taking guns along gathered together, considering a protest. If they all refused to travel under such circumstances then surely the project couldn't continue. They all considered this option. Lee and Claudia consulted alone together. They had already decided not to mention the gunplay in the shopping mall.

Charlie spoke up, 'We're forgetting that we are actually going to the Wild West. Some people were unarmed. But others routinely carried firearms, We're either embracing this game or we're not.'

This conversation was taking place while the others were happily blasting off their Colts and Winchesters. Slowly, Charlie's point of view took hold.

'I suppose you're right,' said Devin.

Claudia just shrugged and turned into Lee's arms. Lee looked back over her head – actually he wanted his own cowboy gun and holster, with the string around the thigh, just like when he was twelve or thirteen years old. He saw Leland buckling up his gun belt and putting his Colt in and out of the holster. The Doc was examining his own special shoulder holster, apparently the way Doc Holliday wore it. A giddy Kevin was working the action of an empty Winchester rifle.

Perhaps aware of how contentious the guns would prove to be, Frankie and Carly only then put in an appearance. They went to the pro-gun lobby first, complimenting each man on how good they looked. 'How jealous am I?' Frankie told them. 'I wish I was going off with you guys. But, for God's sake, be careful with those things. We didn't half agonise over that decision, I can tell you!' The last sentence was pronounced loudly, as a way of appeasing the others as he moved across to them. He was relieved that they seemed ready to accept the situation. Charlie was nearest to him. 'It's the Constitution, Charlie. The right to bear arms, and all that.'

'I understand, Frankie. Like you say, we are in America.'

Leila stood to the side, watching Jon, who was delighted with his new toy. She wanted her own cowboy gun, thought it unfair that she was excluded.

Kevin moved by Leila, looking her up and down. 'Whip

crack away!' he exclaimed.

'Fuck off, dickhead.'

Kevin threw up his hands in mock defence. 'Whoa! Hey, girl, just a Calamity Jane gag.'

Leila ignored him and he went away. She was remembering shooting robotic zombies from the roof of the shopping mall. She looked at Lee, who had Claudia all over him. Melancholy drifted over her for a second, until Charlie approached and punched her lightly on the arm and rolled his eyes at the bizarre situation they found themselves in.

Zac had come across to Lee. 'Hello, there. I've got this for you.' He offered a long-barrelled pistol. 'It's a Colt Walker pistol. It might not be entirely historically accurate, but it's the best we could get.' He gave Lee a black holster stamped with big US letters.

Lee looked at Claudia, who made an expression as if to say she didn't care any more. Lee took the gun and holster and nodded his thanks to Zac.

They sat around inside the warehouse eating Domino's pizza and drinking bottled water. Departure time was almost upon them, so people had become quiet, a few still coming to terms with the day's stunning developments. Charlie had cause to admonish Leland and Kurt for playing with their guns during the meal. It led to a frank *clear the air* talk – basically, the guns were not toys, the time would surely come when they could be used, but until then they should be treated with total seriousness, and consideration given to the people who were wary of them. Lee caressed the wooden stock of his cavalry pistol with the butt of his hand, then closed up the holster, which sat back to front on his left hip.

As Frankie and Carly appeared in a side doorway, with "are we ready?" looks on their faces, Lee took hold of Claudia's hand. 'I'll look after you for every second,' he told her. They kissed, then followed everyone else by getting to their feet.

Some put on their hats, some adjusted holsters, Kurt decided to discard his chaps and went without them. They headed out into bright sunshine. Excited talking replaced the sombre mood. Kevin loudly repeated his opinion on the lack of totty for the trip. Everyone stepped onto a concrete railway platform and fanned out. They were all flabbergasted to be faced with a genuine, fantastic, Wild West train, with the huge black engine, dark smoke already spewing out from the funnel. The driver, in his stripy shirt, grey cap, and red neckerchief, leant out of the cab, looking at them with mild disinterest. Behind him, a stoker was feeding the boiler with logs from the connected wagon. Behind that was a single, beautifully ornate, green-liveried passenger carriage, with a dozen windows.

'Oh, my word!' said Michelle.

'Well, this is it!' cried Frankie. 'Are you ready? All aboard!'

Leila found herself next to Jon for the first time since Chicago. He had not been ignoring her, just experiencing the whole thing and interacting with everybody. He was laughing at the latest surprise. He leant in close to tell her something and inadvertently brushed his lips against her left ear. 'Can you believe this, Leila? Come on, let's be first on.'

He stepped up at the front of the carriage, then reached back to assist her. Devin did the same for Michelle. Lee followed suit with Claudia. Kevin jokingly gave Andy a helping hand. Everyone else boarded, and the people who had chosen to sit on the port side looked through the open windows and bade farewell to Frankie and Carly.

'Michelle, have a good time,' called Frankie. 'Jon, look after Leila.' He stepped forward and shook Charlie's offered hand. 'Take care, Charlie. 'Bye, Kevin.'

The driver blew his whistle.

'Wait for us! Wait for us!'

The heads in the windows swivelled to see two young women, both in their mid-twenties, hurrying along the platform, dressed in gaudy outfits and lace-up boots, with tiny hats on their bouffant hairstyles. Both carried little parasols which they closed shut on reaching the carriage.

'We didn't think you'd make it,' said Frankie.

'Sorry to be a nuisance,' said the brunette of the two women.

She was an incredibly pretty Asian woman with perfect skin and a bright smile for Frankie.

'Shall we get on?' asked the blonde woman, who was equally attractive.

'Go for it,' said Frankie, 'and have a wonderful time.'

The two women climbed aboard as the driver blew his whistle again.

Kevin said to Frankie with a smile, 'I take back my lack of totty comment.'

'Good man!'

The train moved slowly away from the platform.

EIGHT

Everybody naturally stared at the two extra passengers, especially Claudia. She noted that the women sat down at the front of the carriage and began a conversation between themselves before even acknowledging the other people, or offering to introduce themselves. Claudia found that rude and rather suspect. She turned to Lee. 'What do we think of surprise inclusions?'

He thought of the man who had come late into the group in Berkshire, Andrew Scholes, who proved to be Michael Hester's (ultimately violent) sleeper agent – one of the men Lee had been forced to kill. 'We don't like it.'

Finally, the blonde stood up and turned. 'Hello, everyone. We missed Chicago, I'm afraid. We're along for the ride. I'm Gloria Snodgrass and this is Prodilyn Gante.' They were hailed from the length of the carriage. 'I hope we can catch up with you all on the journey.'

Jon and Lee looked at each other and both mimed, with puzzled expressions, "Prodilyn?"

Leila was as displeased as Claudia. The two new women were very sexy and she could sense Jon beside her, craning his neck to take a good look at them.

'That's a turn-up for the books,' he said, as uncommitted as possible, while settling back down.

'Yes, isn't it just.'

Leila looked outside, the remnants of the unknown town slipping behind them and woodland approaching on the left. She heard Kevin get confirmation from Andy that they were heading west again, then Leland state that it was obvious as they were going to the Wild West, and some people laughing. She looked at the women up front again with mistrust, then checked herself and remembered that she had Jon alongside her.

'I'm really nervous,' he suddenly said. 'This is just insane.'

'I'm telling you, this is an improvement. We went by coach last time.'

They trundled west into the low sun. Some people chatted, some slept. Lee had Claudia leaning into him. They had eaten two cereal bars from their own supply and finished the bottled water. For an hour or so they had listened to music on the iPod, before settling in to just watch the vast countryside pass by, with the occasional farm or building on the horizon.

Lee remembered a childhood game, where he would pretend the stairs in the hallway of his family home were a Royal Navy gunboat steaming up the Yangtze or the Nile, and through the wide gaps to the side (somebody had kicked out some of the spindles; it was a rough home) he would shoot his toy Lee Enfield rifle or his cowboy gun at the fleeting images of rebels on the far bank. Then he would have to sling the rifle on his back and climb out and up to the next opening to check on a wounded colleague, making sure not to drop onto the watery carpet below. He watched the ground moving alongside the train, and so wanted to fire his cavalry pistol off into the long grass.

The latecomers, Prodilyn and Gloria, were holding court at the front of the carriage, talking with Kurt, Leland and Devin and Michelle. It was bizarre watching the two women chat and flirt while encased in their period costumes. Word had filtered down that they were from London, had missed their flight. Both were unmarried, and not short of a bob or two. What Prodilyn did for a living was unclear, but Gloria owned a chain of beauty salons, which helped to explain why they were groomed to within an inch of their lives. Claudia had picked up on their appearance. 'I'd like to see what they look like in a couple of months,' she said to Lee.

'Now you mention it,' he said, 'I was thinking just that about you. Last time out you got a bit grungy.'

She slapped his leg. 'I did not! I showered every day. And what products couldn't we get hold of, just by walking to the shops? This is going to be different, though.'

'I suppose it is. No showers where we're going.'

'What will we do?'

'Must be a metal tub near the fire.'

'God, sounds like my Granny's childhood in Yorkshire.'

'No, listen, think about it, I'll heat up some water, you'll sit naked in the bath and I'll pour it all over you. Once a week.'

'Once a week?'

'That could be my job. Bathhouse attendant. You can be Tuesdays, Prodilyn, Wednesdays, Gloria...'

She looked at him with squinted eyes. 'Don't even think about it.'

Leila was sitting between Charlie and Jon, the former asleep and the latter refusing to let her handle his gun. She was chewing away on the first of her supply of gum.

'Ah, go on, Jon.'

'No.'

'I thought you liked me?'

'I do like you.'

'More than the new girls? "Ooh, Jon, isn't this exciting? Here's me, a normal girl from near London, thrown into all this."'

'Prodilyn doesn't talk like that.'

'That was my Gloria impression. What a bimbo!'

'You know I've only got eyes for you, Leila.'

'Do you want to have sex?'

Charlie chuntered in his dreams. Jon admonished Leila with wide eyes and she said, 'Sorry, I'll behave.'

She gave him some gum and they sat listening to the rhythmic rumble of the wheels on the track and feeling the movement of the train. Jon looked about him. Ruth was flat out, asleep. Andy was talking with Phil, with Doc just behind them, listening while looking at the countryside. Lee looked forward as Prodilyn laughed at one of Kevin's jokes. She had striking cheekbones under flawless skin, and perfect teeth, while Gloria was the pale-lipped, equally pure-faced blonde. It puzzled him that they said they were from London. As far as he knew, the target areas had been Blackpool, somewhere north of New York and the Chicago area.

The train was coming to a stop.

Everyone except Ruth got down to stretch their legs. They were stopping to take on water, something that interested Leland and mechanic, Kurt. They stood talking to the driver and his stoker as they watched the filling procedure from a wooden water tower, complete with a squeaky windmill on the top.

Leila and Claudia came together to talk, as a chilly wind flowed across them. They were in the middle of nowhere and the wide open vistas enthralled both of them equally.

'In the family tree research I did,' said Claudia, 'a female ancestor of mine, who emigrated to America, went this way in a wagon train. I believe Indians tried to buy her and she had to hide away.'

'Can you sense what she must have felt out here?'

'I think I can, actually. What an incredibly beautiful place.'

'Do you think this is Texas?'

'It must be, surely.'

They watched some of the men disappear into nearby scrub-land to relieve themselves.

'We'd better... as well,' said Claudia.

'Yeah, you're right. Long journey ahead.'

They wandered off a little further back behind the train.

Lee jogged back to the train, and was engaged in conversation by Prodilyn. They covered the weather, and their extraordinary mode of transport, before he had chance to bring up the subject of her unusual name.

'It's one I've never heard of before,' he said. 'In fact, I don't think any English person would have done. What are the origins of it?'

'Well, let's see. I'm Filipino. We're generally a mix of

different races. I, for one, am half Hispanic-Malay, half Romanian.'

'Good grief.'

'My name came from the word fleur-de-lis, meaning lily flower. My grandmamma was quite fond of French decorations during her time, so my mum named me after one, in honour of her; only she altered the word to make it one of a kind. She used "pro" for superiority and "lyn" for femininity.'

Well, that told me, thought Lee, eyes wide.

When Claudia and Leila came skipping back up the slight incline to the track, they found Lee still talking with Prodilyn. The woman turned to them with a friendly expression on her face. Lee could see that both girls were less than delighted, but they exchanged pleasantries nicely enough. They talked about their outfits and where they were all from.

'I believe you've done something like this before,' Prodilyn suddenly came out with. 'Tell me, what can I expect from these robotic zombies everyone keeps telling me we'll experience?'

'Well,' said Claudia, 'we wouldn't want to spoil the surprise. Just don't let them grab you.'

'No,' put in Lee, 'they'll chew your shoes off. They're not bad, really. Just stay away from them.'

'I'll certainly do that. I hope we can all be friends during this.'

The train whistle sounding allowed Leila and Claudia to avoid replying.

'We'd better get aboard,' said Lee.

They joined a queue to climb back up to the carriage, Lee offering a hand to Prodilyn because of her heavy dress, and receiving dirty looks from both Leila and Claudia. The train moved off immediately. When it was up to about 10 mph there came a shout from Leland, pointing through a window. Ruth came running from the scrub-land. Kevin and Andy jumped to the stairs to help the lady aboard. She thanked them before slumping down on the nearest bench, puffing and blowing.

Michelle reached across to her with a smile. 'We almost lost you there, Ruth.'

They were losing the light. The train stopped again, for no apparent reason.

'This is the longest fucking day of my life,' Kurt suddenly said.

For most of them it was the first time they had heard the Swede speak. It prompted laughter from all the tired people in the carriage. The train sat there in the growing gloom. Then three horse-drawn open wagons came into view. The men on the starboard side of the carriage dropped the windows.

'What now?' asked Phil. 'Are we to go on in those? At night?'

Two of the wagons were driven by men: real cowboys. The third by a middle-aged woman. She stood up on the buckboard and hailed them.

'Hello, there! I'm Barbra. You're all to stay at my ranch tonight.'

NINE

Lee woke up and tried to remember where he was. He looked to the next bed and saw the naked torso of a large black man, snoring loudly. Was he in jail? Then he remembered arriving at the ranch in pitch darkness and having a great supper in the kitchen, laid on by Barbra and her cook, then crashing out in the bunkhouse with the other guys – Claudia bedded down somewhere else with the women.

He thought the place was probably a dude ranch, Barbra being a larger than life character, very much the matriarchal type of woman who could probably ride and rope better than the men. He pulled on his cavalry uniform, already conscious that he felt grimy and in need of a shower. Leland was getting dressed nearby, buttoning his shirt, then it was time for the gun belt, positioned on his hips with great care and pride.

Kevin sat up in his bed. 'Is it breakfast time, chaps? Wonder if we'll be having grits?'

Lee found a lavatory, then went in search of the ranch house from the previous night. There was a fierce, cold wind blowing. Phil, holding his jacket closed and his Derby hat in place, seemed to know where he was going, so Lee followed him. They stepped into a large, high-ceiling communal dining room, all wood and mounted cow horns, then followed the sound of conversation into a warm kitchen, where they found Ruth and Doc drinking coffee at a wooden table, with Michelle helping to provide breakfast with ranch owner, Barbra.

'Sit yourselves down, gentlemen,' said Barbra, smiling broadly. 'Have some coffee.'

Lee and Phil sat, bidding good morning to Ruth and Doc. Barbra placed down two tin cups on the table and poured thick black coffee from a heavy pot. Lee and Phil exchanged a look, both wondering about milk and sugar.

'It's an acquired taste,' whispered Doc. 'The Old West, remember. Better get used to it.'

'No one else up yet, Doc?' asked Lee.

'Some of the ladies went over to see the horses. Claudia amongst them, I believe.'

Phil suggested to Lee, 'Maybe your young lady had a pony when she was growing up.'

'Perhaps she did. But she's not having a horse now she's all grown up.'

They paused while Barbra served Ruth and Doc with plates of bacon, egg and huge pancakes. Lee didn't know what grits were, but they certainly weren't there.

'So, Lee,' continued Phil. 'We've not had chance to talk, yet. How come you were in New Milford?'

'Claudia has relatives there. Good a place as any, I suppose. And you, is it your home town?'

'I'm from Michigan, originally. Been in New Milford for about the last twenty years. It was my late wife's family home.' Phil saw the fresh concern on Lee's face. 'Oh, no, she was taken by cancer, a couple of years before the trouble.' He tried the treacly coffee and grimaced. 'I like that you chose the cavalry outfit. I've been thinking about all my favourite cowboy movies since the Chicago hotel.'

'A fan of Westerns, eh? Didn't consider strapping on some iron?'

'No, no. Too old and set in my ways for that. I see myself as a town elder.'

Lee smiled. They looked to the other two, but the conversation had stopped with the coming of the food. To Lee, Ruth seemed a very introverted person anyway.

Leila came in, yawning in a very unladylike fashion. She paused on seeing Lee. Phil stood to a window to check the view.

'Hi, there, young lady!' called Barbra. 'Want some coffee?'

'Yes, please. Thank you very much.'

Leila took Phil's place. She ignored Doc and Ruth, mimed a "hi" to Lee.

'Sleep well?' he asked her.

'Not really. Claudia snores.' They both laughed. 'No, she doesn't. The bed was like a bag of spanners, though.'

'You look amazing,' he told her.

'I feel terrible.'

'The coffee here will either kill you or cure you.'

Lee experienced a strange sense of déjà vu as he walked out to find Claudia. It made him break his stride – bizarre really, having only ever set foot on the eastern seaboard of America in his entire life. Maybe one of those ancestors Claudia was always banging on about had reached this far west, his great-

great grandfather perhaps, out gold prospecting or gambling in Tombstone, before eventually returning to England. Then when he saw Claudia talking over a fence rail with no less than four real cowboys, he had a flashback to his former Liverpudlian girlfriend, Rachel, in a city centre pub with five suitors around her. He did what he had done that time, he walked up behind Claudia and held her from behind, staking his claim. She sighed back into him. He kissed her neck.

'I leave you for one night and...' he kidded.

'I missed you.'

The cowboys had transferred their full attention to Prodilyn and Gloria. The Londoners had on thick sheepskin coats. Claudia was in a borrowed sweater.

'Look at the horses, Lee,' said Claudia. 'Aren't they beautiful?'

Lee gave the animals some consideration, out in their paddock. 'Yes, magnificent. Which one are you riding back to the train?'

Claudia swivelled in his arms, thrilled. 'Are we doing that? Have they said that?'

'Sorry,' he replied, guiltily. 'It was just a joke.'

'You! When are we leaving?'

'Very soon. Not far now, I believe. A couple of hours. Just a few hills to negotiate, then we're there.'

Gloria turned to face Lee. 'Excuse me, did you say we're off soon?'

Without make-up she was just as attractive. He thought she must have been a model before putting her money into her salons. Lee loved Claudia, but there was no chore in having to look at Miss Gloria Snodgrass for the next six months.

'Yeah, we're going soon,' he answered. 'Come in when you're ready.'

'Okay, Lee. Thank you.'

Lee always felt slightly uncomfortable whenever someone addressed him by name without ever really being introduced. He and Claudia turned and headed back towards the ranch buildings.

'I didn't expect you to be hanging out with those two,' he said.

'Barbra suggested I go with them. I couldn't be rude. I suppose they're all right.'

'There you go, everyone is all right on this trip. It'll be gravy, you'll see.'

Following breakfast, Doc and Kurt had both had the same idea, to drift away from the ranch house without being observed, in order to get into character and practise their quick draws. When they realised they were behind the same barn, albeit eighty feet apart, they acknowledged one another, Kurt laughing, and Doc touching the brim of his black hat. They went through their techniques, Kurt drawing against his own shadow. Doc found it awkward drawing from under his ribcage. But he persisted, building up speed, enjoying himself, pretending it was a life or death situation – then he drew and accidentally fired a bullet into the side of the barn. He jumped back in alarm, before looking guiltily over at Kurt. Both men holstered their weapons and shuffled away in opposite directions.

Barbra and her two cowboys waved them all off as the train got going again with a ridiculous amount of black smoke. They had taken out with them in the open wagons two large baskets of food, which were for their first night inside the fort. 'Fortnum and Mason', Charlie had joked, but Barbra hadn't understood him. Most people waved through the open windows, before settling down in almost the same seats as the day before.

There was early conversation and banter up and down the carriage. Only Ruth continued to keep herself to herself. In the ranch bunkhouse the night before, the women had tried to talk to her, but she was not for turning.

Kevin was the first person to think of going onto the rear footplate to watch the tracks recede into the distance. He opened the door and stopped dead. Doc leant from the right and Lee leant from the left, and the three of them marvelled at the Gatling gun sitting there.

'Bloody hell,' exclaimed Kevin. 'Do you think it's real? It must be.'

Lee, Doc and Phil stood to the doorway.

'Shall we try it?' asked Doc.

'Better not,' suggested Phil. 'We don't want to scare the ladies.'

Kevin fondled the brass stock of the gun, leant around it to see the barrels, then returned to his seat. 'Whoa, this is getting heavy.'

Lee stayed out on the footplate watching the countryside go by. Claudia joined him, pulled a puzzled expression at the machine-gun, then kissed him as he draped an arm around her shoulders.

'Should be there soon,' he told her. 'Are you excited?'
'Bit bored, actually.'
'Bored? But you've got me from the start this time.'
'That's what I meant. Is this the caboose? Phil said the back of the train was the caboose.'
'No, I think a caboose is a separate carriage at the back of a train.'
'That's a shame, I wanted you to kiss me on the caboose.'

The terrain started to rise. The train initially kept its pace up but then there was a noticeable down change. All the windows were closed to a cold morning and nobody seemed to be watching the countryside any more; they just wanted to get to their destination. Lee looked around his companions – if they struggled with a long train journey, then how would they fare with months of 19th century confinement? Kurt looked about ready to explode already. Lee remembered the boy's "longest day of his life" comment and smiled.

Gloria suddenly screamed at the top of her voice and scared the living daylights out of everyone, especially those who had been asleep. She was on her feet, clearly distressed, pointing backwards with both hands to either side of the train, like an air hostess having a bad episode. The younger men reacted by jumping to their feet. Leila, Claudia and Prodilyn were swivelled in their seats trying to understand what was happening.

Everyone seemed to get it at the same time; shouts rose up, curses were spat, Michelle hid her considerable bulk behind her husband's considerable bulk, Gloria and Prodilyn embraced, Lee reached for Claudia. Encroaching on the slow-moving train, filling the view from each window, were dozens of wretched, ragged, bloodstained, pale-faced, shuffling robotic zombies. Although everyone on the train knew the name of the game, it was still an astonishing and pulse-racing sight to see the concerted assault, especially coming at a time when they had their guard down. The zombies kept coming, until they were at the train, their heads and shoulders at the windows, and kept coming until their faces started to smash against the glass. Michelle screamed next, as the first pane of glass came in.

It was Andy who took charge, drawing his Colt pistol to fire at point blank rage through the broken pane, blasting the top of the zombie's head off. Further female wailing accompanied the men's call to arms, Andy waving Kurt, Doc and Leland to his side of the carriage, while directing Lee, Kevin, Devin and Jon to the other. What followed was a cacophony of gunfire, each man delighting in his own way the drawing of his gun and the blasting away through glass at the scary threat.

Smoke accompanied the noise. Zombies were downed on both sides, but others kept coming, gruesome and remarkably rabid. Kurt remembered where one of the Winchester rifles was and brought it into the fray. It was, of course, like shooting fish in a barrel, and it became a massacre when Kevin ran out of bullets for his Colt and decided to bring the Gatling gun into action. He cranked the handle and pulled to the left and right, causing devastating wreckage in the things, thinning them out and creating space between them and the train.

The train levelled out and pulled clear of the attackers.

The gunfire slowed, then ceased. But the men's pumping hearts continued to flood with adrenalin. Through the gun smoke they looked at one another. The ones with partners went to their women folk; Devin found a crying Michelle, Lee embraced a shocked Claudia. Even Jon looked to see how Leila was feeling – she was wide-eyed and stunned.

Slowly the situation stabilised and people sat down. Charlie and Phil moved about, distributing bottles of water to the gunmen. Kurt summed it up for all of them, 'This is the craziest train journey ever in my life.'

The train stopped – not something any of the passengers were happy with after what had just happened. They all waited to find out the reason why.

'Maybe another water stop,' suggested Devin.

Since the zombie attack, Lee had done two definite things: lovingly and slowly reloaded his gun and lovingly and slowly snogged Claudia. He felt like a real gunfighter; he had lived out that childhood game of shooting from the gunboat on the Yangtze. 'I need to fuck you,' he whispered to Claudia.

She laughed. 'Where do you suggest we do that? The roof?'

Of the others, Doc felt the most pride in his part in defending the train. He sat with his legs crossed, conscious of his shoulder holster cutting into his ribs. He tidied his waistcoat and adjusted his neck tie. His wife back in Chicago flashed into his mind. She was safe with her family, but he missed her dreadfully already. He was first to see the train driver walking back along the side of the track to speak with them.

'Folks,' said the driver. 'Are you all okay back here? Nobody hurt? We have a little problem, be only a few minutes. Maybe you'd all like to stretch your legs?'

Everyone got off the train, a little warily. At least there was no imminent threat of another attack as they had come to a stop between two rock faces. The dark smoke from the stack was being blown forward, drifting over a covered wooden bridge. Jon moved alongside Lee. 'Lee, if that's a rickety bridge and we have to walk over it in single file, I think I've seen that film.'

'Kenneth More? Northwest Frontier?'

'That's the one.'

'How many zombies did you get back there?'

'At least seven.'

'Wicked, wasn't it?'

Leila appeared between her two favourite men. 'Boys, are they ever going to get us anywhere, or will we just ride this train for six months?'

'Leila,' said Jon, 'I promise you there'll come a time in the fort when you'll actually beg to be on this train.'

'Let's go and check out that bridge,' said Lee. 'Leila, are you coming along?'

'Might as well. I need a pee, anyway.'

TEN

The rickety bridge proved to be a red herring, and they were soon crossing it and steaming onwards. The driver had mentioned to someone that it was now the last leg coming up, so everyone was cheered by that news. They went for about thirty minutes through fairly hilly terrain, before they stopped once more. Kurt swore loudly.

After a minute, the driver came back to them again. 'Sorry about this, people. The track's damaged up ahead.'

Lee looked at Jon as they both mouthed, '*Northwest Frontier.*'

'Could be *Von Ryan's Express*, perhaps?' said Lee. 'Happened in that film too.'

The driver trotted away. After a moment, some of the men stirred from their seats to check out the problem for themselves. Lee, Jon, Andy and Kevin walked forward, on past the engine, joining the driver and the stoker in looking down at a single buckled piece of rail.

'You have tools, of course?' Jon asked the driver. 'Can't we replace the broken track with one from behind the train?'

Lee watched the driver's face carefully to see if that had been the plan all along, but the man showed no emotion and seemed to be seriously giving it some thought.

'Let's do it!' said the driver.

Kevin smiled ruefully at everyone. 'Now it's manual labour, is it? This wasn't in the brochure.'

'No, Kevin, listen,' said Jon. 'We'll have to split the manpower, one group replaces the track, while the other provides cover.'

'From fresh zombie attack, you mean?'

'Exactly. Why don't you and Andy organise some defence, while me and Lee put a team together to move the rails?'

Kevin loved that idea. 'Come on, Andy. Let's get on it.'

They went back down the train.

'Always good to be volunteered,' joked Lee.

'Keeps him happy. Who do we need?'

'Devin, of course. You, me and Leland should cover it with the driver and stoker.'

'You get them, I'll arrange the tools.'

Lee walked back. Leila was sticking her head out of a window.

'What's up?' she asked.

'Don't be nosey.' He jumped up into the carriage. 'Everyone, we have to swap a piece of rail from behind the train with a damaged one up ahead. Devin, will you help?'

Devin got up immediately. Lee saw that Leland and Kurt were already checking the Winchesters with Kevin – of course, the boys would want to defend the train. Charlie and Phil got to their feet without being asked. Lee didn't insult the elder statesmen by refusing their help.

The navvies disembarked, Lee sending them forward to Jon. Leila was out of the window again. 'Lee,' she called.

'Leave me your gun.' He tried to object. 'Come on, man, it's 2018. It's not fair I can't help.'

He took his Colt from its holster and passed it up. 'Be very careful.'

She winked at him. Lee headed to the front of the train.

Kurt went up onto the top of the carriage with one of the rifles and a box of shells. Andy stayed on the footplate between carriage and fuel tender. Kevin manned the Gatling gun. Leland stayed inside. He noticed Leila was primed and ready with the handgun.

'Whip crack away!' he said to her.

'Don't you start as well!'

Then she smiled at him.

Up ahead, heavy tools were handed out and the driver showed them where to stand and what to do. Lee shared another look with Jon as he started to open up a bolt. In the film, *Northwest Frontier,* the train came under attack from rebel tribesmen with rifles – the zombies were not likely to be shooting at them, but it was still a tense time. They both checked the undulating terrain either side of the track. It appeared all clear, so far. Everyone worked hard and fast. It was quite cold but they soon built up a sweat.

'Almost there,' said the stoker, working his own bolt.

They got the bent rail loose, threw down their tools and lined up along its length. Jon organised the lift, on three, and they had it up and staggered off to the side, where it was deposited.

'Good job,' said Lee. 'Off we go behind the train.'

They trooped past Leila's side. When her head appeared once more, Lee shouted in jest, 'Get in! Stupid woman.'

'We've got you covered,' she replied.

The driver chose a rail behind the track, which they went to work on. Shots suddenly rang out from the train and they all froze over their work. They could see Kurt firing the Winchester from the roof of the carriage.

'Come on,' said Lee. 'Let's keep at it!'

Kurt had seen a group of shambolic zombies rise out of a gulley on the left side of the train. He put down two with the first three shots fired and was absolutely delighted – the craziest train journey of his life just got better and better. He fired again, and heard more rifle fire from inside the carriage. Then there were pistol shots, but going out to the other side, so he spun round and saw many more zombies staggering forward from that direction. He fired and fired until he had to kneel down and reload.

As Prodilyn, Gloria, Claudia and Michelle ducked for cover (Ruth just sat there impassively), Leila fired the Colt through the open window. It gave her a tremendous thrill, actually made her giddy, knowing her shots were hitting the humanoid shapes coming up out of shrubbery and from around rocks. None seemed to have fallen, but she was trying her best, nevertheless.

There came a short burst from Kevin on the Gatling gun, but his angles were all wrong, so he abandoned the machine-gun and dropped to the track. He drew his pistol and shot down the nearest zombie in one movement. 'Fucking A!' Then he held fire as the men with the new rail came by. 'Watch out!' he called to the fighters on the train. 'Men passing! Men passing!'

As he staggered along with his share of the metal, Lee

managed to glance up at Leila. She made him proud, going at it like a good 'un. The six of them crabbed sideways towards the gap in the track. Andy jumped down and stayed with them, offering cover. His expression didn't change, he just kept picking off the zombies, pausing to reload from the bullets in his belt, then going again. The rail was positioned and bolted in place.

'That'll do!' shouted the driver, drenched in sweat. 'Get aboard, everyone!'

The tools were thrown aside and they made for the carriage, Andy bringing up the rear. Prodilyn and Gloria helped the men aboard, where they collapsed on the floor. Gunfire continued. It seemed an age before the train moved off, but it did, so Kevin cheered and Leila screamed with laughter. She tried to fire the Colt one more time but only got an empty click. They had forgotten Kurt on the roof. Michelle shouted when she saw the Winchester being handed down, Lee grabbed it, then Kurt swung himself in through a window, much to the admiration of the women.

The mood was celebratory as the train got back up to speed, cooling air flooding through the open windows to revive the exhausted men. Claudia passed around what was left of the bottled water. She checked Lee was all right. They sat down, Lee breathing deeply.

'Bloody hell,' he said to her, smiling. 'Bit different to the Berkshire trip.'

Fed up already with their heavy clothes and little hats, Prodilyn and Gloria sat on their bench as the train rattled along, talking quietly about the others. They found Kurt cute, of course, with his blond Scandinavian looks and sullen mood. He had impressed Gloria, particularly, by being on the roof of the carriage during the last zombie attack. Prodilyn liked the look of Leland. She had more of an association with America than Gloria, and found Leland's accent to be very soothing. They both agreed Kevin was a handsome older man, but thought he might become a nuisance with his garrulous personality. They liked Doc's reserved and quiet demeanour. Lee and Jon were in the same bracket: good-looking but with female associations in Claudia and Leila.

'We're only discussing the guys,' laughed Prodilyn. 'What are we like?'

'I know! Go on, then, which one do you choose for the early days? I'll have a go at Kurt.'

'Oh, you got in quick there, babe. All right, Leland will do for starters.'

ELEVEN

It was raining when they got their first view of the fort, as the train came around in a wide curve towards a swollen river. Everyone gathered at the windows on the right hand side of the carriage, to see the dark, brooding mass of wood, appearing black in the downpour, with prominent, overhanging square defensive positions above the central gate area, as well as at the three visible corners. Over the gatehouse hung two limp flags, one for the State of Texas and the other the Stars and Stripes. It didn't look much like Kevin's fort from his childhood; it seemed much earlier than that, very rustic, very basic and very grim. It covered a large area and filled the horizon up to the low, foreboding cloud cover.

'Shit,' said Kurt, adding to his quota of words for the trip.

'Some place,' said Devin, whistling.

'Clearly, though,' said Charlie, 'it's not under zombie siege.'

'Maybe they're all inside,' suggested Prodilyn. 'Will you clean them out for us, Kurt?'

Kurt nodded. Gloria laughed.

'Is it the fucking Alamo?' asked Kevin. 'Sorry, all you

Americans. I know how defensive you are about that place, especially that time when Ozzy Osbourne pissed on it.'

The train levelled out, going straight for the main gate. Lee and Jon looked at each other and laughed; in *Northwest Frontier* the train smashes through the outer gate of a fort. But the gates were open to receive their slowing train, and it came to a stop perfectly in the middle of the compound. The gates closed behind it. The train sat there, huffing and puffing.

'Well?' asked Prodilyn, after a moment. 'Shall we get out?'

'We might as well,' answered Michelle.

Everyone stepped down to the muddy earth, some of the ladies lifting the hems of their skirts. Cowgirl Leila didn't have that problem, so skipped away from the train, straining to see where she was, as rain pattered onto her cowboy hat. To her left, near the front wall, there seemed to be a stable block. Next to that, some kind of office, made of heavy horizontal logs, and then another official building, bigger but less intimidating, as if there were living quarters inside as well. To the right, a large building, with smoke rising from a black metal chimney: the kitchen, maybe. She looked through the train windows and out the other side, to an even larger building, stretching from midway along the side wall to the front. Jon was beside her.

'Let's see about getting in out of the rain,' he said. 'We can investigate later.'

Michelle and Devin moved towards the smoke, as the kitchen was going to be their territory. Everyone drifted after them. The driver came walking back, avoiding puddles, to check everyone had left the train.

'Have we got the Winchesters?' called Kevin.

'Yep!' answered Leland.

'The provisions from the ranch?' asked Andy.

'Yes!' said Devin.

'Have we got Ruth?' asked Claudia.

'Nope!' said Charlie.

Everyone saw the far gate open with a flash of clear sky to the west. Clearly the train was leaving them very soon. Claudia and Michelle went back aboard. Ruth was still sitting in exactly the same spot, her face completely impassive.

'Ruth, honey,' called Michelle. 'We're here, girl.'

No response. Claudia tried. 'Ruth, are you all right?'

Both women came towards Ruth; she smiled up at them.

'I'm not going to be staying,' she told them.

'Why not?' asked Claudia. 'It might seem crazy now, but it should settle down.' Thinking of Berkshire, she couldn't believe what she was saying.

'Thank you, Claudia. My mind's made up. I'll stay on and ride to the next town.'

Michelle looked at Claudia, who shrugged.

'If you're sure,' said Michelle.

'Very sure, thank you, Michelle.'

That was that. They left her there. Claudia told the driver what was happening.

'Can't say I'm surprised,' he said. 'Thought more of you people would pull out. Tell her two hours further and she'll be met off the train.'

Michelle sourced some supplies and water from her husband, and made sure Ruth had them for her extra journey. She said goodbye and stepped down from the train.

'Let's get in,' said Devin.

The husband and wife team from Chicago led them under cover outside the cookhouse. From there they watched the train move out, Ruth's forward-facing silhouette at one of the windows. It went out through the far gate, that gate closed, and they all considered themselves well and truly delivered.

It was warm and dry inside the large cookhouse, lit by half a dozen hanging kerosene lamps. The large black range cooker was alight in the kitchen, while the other end of the room contained a fireplace, near which were grouped austere wooden seating and tables, although there was one leather chair and a vintage chaise longue. Michelle and Devin did a quick inventory, then set to boiling water for hot drinks, while everyone else sat down. It was clearly a shock to the system to be sitting peacefully in silence. Faces looked about them. They would have to get used to living in wooden rooms. There was a stocked bookcase, a Grandfather clock, a number of framed sepia photographs of hard to make out people, but of most interest, a piano sitting there.

'Piano,' whispered Lee to Claudia. They had somehow ended up on the chaise longue.

'I can't imagine that being used.'

Prodilyn and Gloria took off their hats and discarded them for good. Then they examined their muddy boots on the floorboards, which couldn't be helped, they supposed.

'I'm getting a Glastonbury vibe,' announced Gloria.

'A what?' asked Kurt, in the next chair.

'The Glastonbury music festival. Last time I was there it turned into a muddy quagmire.'

'Were you in a tent?' asked Jon, grinning.

She smiled back at him. 'No fear. I cheated a bit. Corporate hospitality.'

Michelle and Devin were passing out rations from Barbra's ranch.

'So, we've lost Ruth,' said Phil. 'She never seemed quite with it, I must say.'

Gloria had no interest in Ruth. She said, 'If we have a cold winter, this place is going to be unbearable.'

'Where do we sleep?' asked Leland.

'Over the way there,' said Leila. 'There's a big building.'

'Shall we go and see? After we've eaten, I mean.'

'Sure, why not?'

Lee nudged Claudia. 'Wonder what our room is like?'

'You're assuming we're in together. It might be girls and boys. Just kidding! You should see your face – total panic. It can't be any worse than our bedroom in New Milford.'

'True. What are you eating?'

'I've no idea!'

They fell against each other, laughing.

Jon accepted a cup of coffee from Michelle. He couldn't quite believe he was there, couldn't quite believe he was involved in one of these insane events. He watched Leland chatting up Leila, while they had their own coffee. Then she turned to Charlie and asked if he wanted to come with them to check out the sleeping arrangements. Jon grinned at Leland's badly concealed disappointment.

In the end, everyone but Devin and Michelle trooped across to investigate. The heavy clouds had brought on a premature dark, and with some of them being very tired anyway, it wouldn't be long before they crashed out for the night. Leila led the way into the bunkhouse building. Lit kerosene lamps were on little shelves at regular intervals. It was constructed from the heavy horizontal logs, just like the office, and was very rudimentary, but seemed cosy enough. They filed in off the boardwalk. There was one solitary black iron stove in the hallway for the whole building.

'Clearly no en suite bathrooms, I see,' commented Prodilyn.

Each door had a name tag pinned to it. Devin and Michelle had the first room. Everyone looked in: a double bed with a nice Old West patchwork duvet, two bedside tables. On the floor sat two pieces of luggage. All things considered, it was quite suitable. Across the hall was Lee and Claudia's room. They didn't enter until everyone had moved down the hall. Inside, they found themselves faced with bunk beds. Claudia burst out laughing. Lee pulled a face, then they embraced and laughed together. Their bags from Chicago sat there on the floor.

Prodilyn was sharing with Gloria. They pounced on their luggage.

'Bagsy the top bunk,' said Gloria.

Prodilyn tutted. 'You're such a Girl Guide.'

Across from them, Leland was in with Kurt. They didn't bother going into the room, but stayed with the group. Doc with Jon. Kevin with Andy. Phil with Charlie. At the end, Leila found she should have been sharing with Ruth.

'Oh, cool,' she said. 'A room to myself.'

There was laughter out in the hallway.

While all the others returned to the cookhouse, Lee and Claudia stayed behind in their room. Lee claimed the top bunk, and invited Claudia up to join him.

'All right, homber,' she said, climbing up and lying beside him.

'What did you call me?'

'I just remembered, by complete coincidence, one of my dad's favourite films was *Hombre* with Paul Newman. But he always called it homber. And he used to call concrete, corncrete.'

'Didn't you once tell me your dad ran a firm that laid driveways?'

'Yeah, it really used to confuse his clients. He would say to them, "You can have block paving, flagstones or corncrete, love".'

Lee laughed. 'You're so cute, you know. I love you so much.'

'Do you, really? Make love to me, then.'

'I intend to, my good lady. Just as soon as I've been to the loo.'

He made a joke of climbing over her with a big groan and dropped to the floorboards.

'I'll have to go later,' she told him. 'You'll have to tell me where it is.'

'I hadn't planned on keeping it a secret.'

'Lee.' He stopped at the door. 'Why haven't we got a double bed like Devin and Michelle?'

'Because they're married. We're not, you hussy.'

Carrying one of the kerosene lamps, Lee went outside. It had stopped raining, but dusk had fallen. He gambled that the latrines would be nearer the river, heading towards the dark mass in the far right corner. He entered through what appeared to be a bathhouse (the place he was supposed to pour hot water over a naked Claudia in the tub) and found the toilet stalls in the back. They were basic, to say the least. For a moment he thought he was back in his run down high school in England. All the place needed was a fug of cigarette smoke and obscene graffiti on the walls.

He passed Leland on the way out.

'Take this,' said Lee, handing over the lamp. 'You might fall down the shithole in the dark.'

Claudia had unpacked some of their personal items and placed them on their single dresser. Her dress was open at the front, revealing a little cleavage to him on his return.

'Is it all right?' she asked, of the latrines.

'Yes, if you are judging by Egyptian standards.'

'Oh, God.'

He took her in his arms and kissed her neck. 'Do you want to rejoin the others?'

'Not particularly. Shall we go to bed?'

'Your place or mine?'

As their lips came together, he slipped his hands inside the dress to cup her breasts.

'I love this dress,' he told her. 'You will be wearing it again?'

'Of course I will. I've not exactly got a full wardrobe with me here.'

'What have you got on underneath it? Go on, tell me. Original Old West stockings and suspenders?'

'My Adidas leggings.'

He huffed. 'Well, they can be straight off.'

'But Lee, it's getting a bit nippy in here. There's no central heating, you know.'

She then took off the dress. He marvelled at her toned upper body, and then watched the figure-hugging black leggings as she climbed up to the top bunk and got under the blankets with a mock chatter of her teeth. Lee stripped completely and joined her.

'You're right,' he told her, 'it is getting a bit cold. Let me warm you up.'

He moved above her and kissed her neck again, then her lips, moving down to kiss the top of her chest. She was quite skinny, so there was no spare flesh beneath his lips. Her legs naturally opened for him. He was against her. They giggled because of the 21st century item of clothing she still had on.

'You've got me worried now, Lee?'

'About what? I've not even started yet.'

'The toilets. You'll have to take me there later.'

'You're joking, aren't you?'

'No.'

'I'll tell you something, if this was really the 1870's, there'd be a chamber pot in here.'

'No!' She turned her face away with horrified embarrassment.

TWELVE

Somehow, somewhere, a bugle played reveille full blast at sunrise the following morning. It woke up everyone except Lee and Claudia, who remained well away, snuggled up together on the top bunk in their room.

People dressed, shuffled to the latrines, then found themselves in the cookhouse, where Devin and Michelle were already cooking breakfast with the last of Barbra's supplies. Charlie poured himself a cup of black coffee, before addressing the cooks. 'Are we imposing on you two good people?'

'Not at all,' answered Devin. 'Man, we love to cook. Maybe it's why we were chosen, but don't worry, this is our thing.'

'Okay, then.'

Kevin came in. 'Good morning, all. What the hell was that racket?'

Prodilyn and Gloria were sitting there, half asleep on the chaise longue, in jeans and jumpers, their hair loose and tousled. Leland and Kurt were standing around, in full costume. Kevin himself still looked like a cowboy, but was not wearing his gun belt. He helped himself to coffee and wondered whether he preferred the two beautiful women in modern clothes or what they had travelled in. He sat down next to Charlie.

'So,' said Kevin, 'we're here. What do we do now? Should we elect a leader?'

'A leader?' asked Charlie.

'Well, you know, someone to make decisions. For this week, anyway. Then someone else has a go next week. Isn't that what they do in situations like this?'

'I really wouldn't have a clue. Maybe we should have a meeting. Decide on things to be done and on certain rules.'

'Yes, I'll suggest it, when everyone's here.'

Everyone, minus Lee and Claudia, were soon there, tucking into ham and eggs and pancakes, served up on traditional pewter dishes. Once the cooks had sat down with them to eat, Kevin raised the subject of having a meeting.

'What's wrong with now?' asked Andy. 'We'll tell the two sleepyheads what we decided later.'

So they had their first meeting. Nobody was elected leader, but some of the practical matters were dealt with: Devin and Michelle would cook twice a day, morning and evening, assuming they found more food. Leland and Jon volunteered to make sure there was a constant supply of water and firewood to the cookhouse. Leila and Kurt were talked into washing-up duties, for the next couple of days, at least. Doc, who had found his medical bag in his room the night before, would make himself available for the general health of the group. Charlie and Phil would deal with garbage disposal, though exactly how they would accomplish that was still to come to them.

They all agreed to meet in a few days, to swap things

around and add other duties as and when they saw fit.

'And now,' said Kevin. 'Shall we all have a look around the place?'

They split into random groups, moving away from the cookhouse in all directions. Kevin, Andy and Jon headed to the front gate, passing the covered well which they all peered down. They found the gate barred with the heavy horizontal beam of wood in place – Kevin seemed to like that. Jon led the way up one of the ladders and they all climbed into the overhanging defensive blockhouse, empty apart from a rank bad smell and the small amount of light allowed in through the front opening. They all peered at the outside world. Milling about below were a good thirty to forty zombies. Even at a distance they were as unnerving as the ones encountered on the journey in. Kevin turned away from the view and scratched his head. The three men looked at each other in the gloom.

'Under siege,' said Jon.

Kurt and Leland had mounted the walkway which encircled the fort, near the north blockhouse on the side wall, and got their own view of the besieging zombies. Kurt swore for both of them. They considered taking pot shots with their pistols, but felt inhibited after the meeting. They moved along the parapet towards the far wall. From there they had a glorious view of the river, and of the bridge that spanned it. The corners of the fort came to the riverbank on both sides, so no zombies could enter this area. It also created their own private little beach under the bridge approaches, but it was not the time of year for sunbathing or swimming.

Leila found herself wandering with Prodilyn and Gloria

towards the stables and the official looking buildings. They looked in the larger one first, seeing immediately the imposing black and white cow horns mounted on the wall. Below them sat a desk and a couple of leather chairs. There were two wooden filing cabinets and a black stove, with firewood stacked beside it. Through to the back was a single bunk with a porcelain wash basin and jug on a stand.

They moved on to the smaller office. Here they became a bit stuck in the mud and had a giggly time helping each other pull legs free. Then something outside the little building stopped them dead. On a wooden platform, about six foot squared and up seven or eight steps, stood the unmistakable sight of a solitary gallows, together with dangling noose. It was understandable that they hadn't noticed it in the rain the previous night, but it was a shock to them in daylight. Still, they made no comment on it as they checked out the building.

'A jail,' said Gloria, the only one of the three to fully enter the room. 'With two little cells in the back.'

'Oh, right,' said Prodilyn. 'Do you think I'll be able to get Leland locked up in there?'

The two of them laughed. Leila was already moving towards the stable block. She pulled open the double doors to let the light flood in. Obviously there were no horses, but two vehicles sat in there; a fabulous, original, US stagecoach in red livery, and a covered wagon, the kind settlers used to cross the plains, the long front axle tongue sitting on the floor. They were such amazing finds that Prodilyn waved over the boys from the gatehouse and they all went about examining them.

'Fantastic!' exclaimed Kevin, focussing on the stagecoach.

Jon was equally excited by it. 'I've got to get up there.' Laughing, he climbed up via the front wheel and the driver's seat to get on top. 'Look, everyone, I'm Jim Dale, in *Carry on Cowboy*.'

Kevin and Gloria laughed – the only ones to recognise the 1960's British comedy film. Kevin reached to open one of the doors, intending to be a gentleman and help Gloria to sit up inside. She smiled and gave him a dainty curtsey. As he turned the handle and opened the little door something sprang at him, causing him to throw himself back onto the ground with a loud cry of, 'Shit!'

Gloria gasped and stepped back. It was Prodilyn who screamed as she saw the zombie rattlesnake on the floor of the carriage. It was a black snake, coiled around its rattle, its mouth viciously snarling. What, bizarrely, made it even more frightening were the parts of it that were missing at various stages along its length – the zombification process.

Leila pulled the distressed Prodilyn away, as Jon demanded to know what was happening from atop the carriage. Andy took charge, and in one movement stepped forward, drew his Colt and shot the thing through the head.

'Fucking hell,' said Kevin, clasping his chest in mock heart attack fashion, in no rush to get up.

The women left the stables. Leland and Kurt came running in, followed by Charlie, Doc and Phil. Jon leaned over the door frame to take a look at what was left of the zombie snake.

Everyone returned to the comparative safety of the cookhouse. Devin put on a fresh pot of coffee while they all talked through the snake booby trap. Leila stood there watching them. It had not come as a surprise to her, as a number of such things had happened in the Berkshire shopping mall. She suddenly felt quite lonely, wishing Lee would get his arse out of bed and show his face. At least she had Charlie sitting there. She put her arms around his neck and hugged him. He smiled and patted her hands.

'All in the game,' said Doc.

'Sure,' replied Phil. 'What other surprises await us?'

'Starvation, maybe,' answered Michelle. 'The stores are empty. I don't know what we're going to do.'

Every face looked concerned.

'Surely they wouldn't do that to us?' asked Charlie.

'I don't know,' said Devin. 'We've got plenty of biscuits. That's about all.'

Through the next couple of hours some people worried about the food issue, and some people didn't. Kurt was in the latter group, and he went back to bed. Leila and Charlie climbed up to the parapet to look down on the river. Devin and Michelle joined the others as they tentatively returned to the compound. Before the snake attack, Doc, Phil and Charlie had been examining their own discovery. On a spur of rail off the main track sat a handcar, one of those small contraptions that moved along a track by two people using a see-saw action. It was old and rusty. They decided there could not be any practical use for the thing, but it made a nice feature sitting there between the cookhouse and the track.

A strange whistling sound finally roused Lee and Claudia. It was loud, seemingly coming from far off. Lee propped himself up on an elbow and found Claudia's face amidst all her hair.

'What time is it?' she asked, through her befuddled mind.

'Time don't matter any more, girl. Let's get up, I'm starving.'

The whistle came again.

'What's that?' she asked.

'I don't know. Maybe it says, "come and get it".'

'Breakfast, you mean?'

'Mmm.'

'Make love to me again.'

'You must be kidding?'

They had made love long into the early hours. Lee stroked her face, then climbed over her again (he would have to make sure she was against the wall in future) and dropped down. He dressed hurriedly – not that he was cold, just that his stomach hurt from hunger. He found the famous Adidas leggings at the far side of the room and threw them onto her left arm.

'Come on,' he barked.

'Hey, where did all the romance go?' she complained with a lovely smile.

Leila and Charlie were in agreement on how beautiful the river looked, and how nice it would be to get up on the west wall at various times of the coming days to just watch it go by. Especially at sunset.

'I don't see why we can't go out on the bridge occasionally,' said Charlie. 'We're safe enough there.'

'You're forgetting, Charlie, we haven't got any food.'

'That's just a trick. We'll be here for the six months, mark my words. I wonder how it will pan out in here. Have you told anyone about Blackpool yet?'

'No. Leland asked, but I didn't go into detail. I'm not ashamed of it, but maybe people wouldn't understand.'

'I think maybe they would, Leila. Everyone here has been in their own personal squat for the last couple of years. But not to worry. We won't talk about it with anyone, if you don't want to.'

'Thanks, Charlie. Do you think we'll be all right?'

'I don't see why not. We'll find things to occupy our time. Leland, in your case.'

She blushed. 'I don't think so, Charlie.'

'Or Kurt.'

'No.'

'Jon.'

'Jon? Don't even go there.'

'I've seen the way he looks at you. I wish there were still bookmakers in the world. I'd put a tenner on you and Jon.'

'Well, then, you'd lose your money.'

They smiled at each other.

Then the whistle came from far away, and they both looked in the direction it had come from, upriver. Trees on the bank hid the nearest curve of the river.

'Told you,' said Charlie. 'A trick.'

'But what is it?'

'Just wait.'

The whistle came again before anything appeared. Leila looked down into the compound, where inquisitive faces looked up from outside the cookhouse. Then Leila saw a flash of red through the overhanging trees.

'A boat!' she cried. 'A very strange boat.'

It was red and white, with two enormous black funnels at the front.

'Good grief,' said Charlie, shaking his head. 'It's a paddle boat.'

'A what?'

'A paddle steamer. It's got a big paddle at the back pushing it along. How extraordinary.' He turned to the others below. 'A paddle steamer!'

'Supplies,' they all said to each other. 'Food.'

Kurt and Leland scurried up the ladders to see for themselves.

'Will it stop?' Kurt asked Charlie.

'I bloody hope so. It won't get under that bridge. Yes, look, its drifting in to the bank.'

The paddle boat took its time. When it eventually docked, just north of them, it seemed as tall as the fort, even accounting for the fort being on higher ground. There was no great rush of movement on board. In fact, it just sat there.

During this lull, there were numerous calls from ground level for information. Finally, Charlie climbed down the ladder and spoke to the group.

'May I suggest we send a party out to it?'

Lee and Claudia came walking across to them.

'What's happening?' asked Lee.

'A boat just arrived,' called down Leila.

'Oh, hey, you up there!'

'Hey, yourself.'

Phil said to Lee, 'You've slept in, missed the first look-see.'

'Ah, been there, done that. Is there any possibility of breakfast?'

'Biscuits and coffee only, I'm afraid,' replied Jon.

'Really? That's a bit like being at home with Claudia in the kitchen.'

Michelle asked Devin to keep abreast of the supply situation, while she took Lee and Claudia into the cookhouse. Devin wasn't too keen to go outside the walls. It was left to Andy, Jon and an insistent Leila to meet the boat.

While the two boys checked their pistols like true cowboys, Leila ran into her room for her hat. Devin did use his strength to remove the bar to the west gate, and Kurt pulled the doors open.

It was quite muddy down along the bank. Leila held onto Jon a few times as they approached the boat. As they got close, activity began on deck, with crewmen sliding two ramps down onto the shore. A white-haired, bespectacled man, clearly the captain, came to the port rail and hailed them in a jovial fashion.

'How are you? I didn't expect to find anyone here.'

'Hello,' called Andy. 'Have you got something for us?'

'I sure have.'

The paddle boat captain came down one of the ramps and approached to shake all their hands. 'I'm Captain Wallis. So, this is really happening then? Hot damn! You people are braver than me. You're fantastic. Especially you, little lady.'

Leila smiled, thinking this old man was just great.

Andy was about to ask about the supplies, when he was shocked to see four horses being led down the ramps. Instead, he just pointed at them.

'Oh my God!' squealed Leila, delighted.

Captain Wallis beamed with happiness at the sight of the

animals.

'Horses?' asked Andy. 'Well... all right. How about our supplies, Captain? Can your crew help us get them up to the fort?'

'I've no supplies for you, I'm afraid,' answered the Captain. 'Just the horses, and their feed.'

'Are we to eat their feed?' asked Leila. 'Or eat the horses?'

'Lord forbid, young lady! But I've got nothing else. I can give you some provisions from the galley, but it won't be much.'

There was nothing more to be said. The Captain shook their hands again and headed back to check the horses were safely disembarked. Leila hurried after him, excited to meet the horses.

'Bloody horses?' asked Jon of Andy. 'What's that all about?'

'Very strange, I agree. But we'd better take them in. Come on.'

Captain Wallis directed some crewmen to take the horses' feed up to the gate. He then approached Andy and gave him a manila envelope.

'You're to open that after we've gone,' said the captain. 'We'll be back in four weeks. Good luck to you.'

Leila and one other sailor came along the bank with two horses each. Jon, despite being very wary, took the two from the sailor, and the man ran after his captain.

'Leila?' asked Jon, 'Did you happen to have a pony as a little girl?'

'Certainly not. These buggers scare me to death, but aren't they just fucking fab!?'

124

GB Hope

THIRTEEN

The horses were walked into the fort, much to everyone's bewilderment, and tied up outside the cookhouse. Lee was holding Claudia from behind as they drank their coffee on the boardwalk.

'Now, that's interesting,' he said over her left shoulder.

Devin and Leland locked up the gate. Prodilyn and Gloria stroked the horses' necks tentatively, clearly neither of them with very much equine experience.

'What's the game, Andy?' asked Kevin. 'Where's the supplies? We can't stay here without food.'

Andy waved the manila envelope. 'We might have to work for the supplies. Let's go in and discuss the situation.'

Everyone filed into the cookhouse and sat around. Andy read what was in the envelope to himself. His face, impassive at the best of times, gave nothing away.

'Well?' asked Kevin.

Andy handed him the contents of the envelope, which included a map. 'We have to go out and get our food.'

'Oh, shopping!' said Gloria, to some titters.

Charlie asked, 'On horseback? Can anyone here ride?'

'I can,' said Prodilyn. 'But I don't want to go out the front there.'

'I'm okay with horses,' said Leland.

'It's not riding,' said Kevin, looking up from the papers. 'It's the stagecoach.'

Charlie stood and walked off. 'That's worse.'

Lee and Claudia were listening from the doorway. 'You can handle that,' he said to her. 'With your Pikey roots. Think of it as a Romany caravan.'

'Shush.'

Andy went on to describe what the mission entailed. The horses were to be harnessed to the stagecoach. They would follow the railroad track back the way they had come for approximately five miles. The map would take them to the supply stash.

'May I speak?' asked Phil. 'Who amongst us would be able to do that?'

'I can,' called Claudia.

Lee did a double-take at her. 'I was joking,' he whispered.

'I've worked on my uncle's farm in Yorkshire as a child. I've driven carts.'

'This is nothing like that,' said Lee, quickly becoming concerned. 'This is four horses and a vintage stagecoach. It could roll easily.'

'Lee,' interjected Kevin. 'Someone's got to drive the coach. If not to go for food, then to carry us out of this shithouse.'

Claudia appealed to her boyfriend. 'I think I can do it.'

'But the zombies out there?' put in Michelle.

'Run them down,' said Kevin.

'Kevin,' said Charlie, 'You clearly love your food, mate.'

The "mate" was clearly said strongly, as if he should stop

throwing his weight around, but Kevin laughed it off. 'I do, that's a fact. But this is a critical situation.'

Kurt spoke up, 'If Claudia thinks she can do it, that's good. I'll go, as... what is it called? Shotgun.'

'Me, too,' offered Leland.

'And me,' said Leila.

Lee spun on her. 'You're not going.'

'Why the fuck not? Because I'm a girl? Claudia's a girl.'

It had been the reason, but Lee deflected it away. 'Leave room for the supplies, will you.'

'Don't be ridiculous!' said Leila.

They stared into each other's eyes. A couple of years ago, when they were lovers in England, he would have been wary of her throwing a punch. She seemed a little less volatile these days.

'People!' called Kevin. 'If it's on, let's put a plan together. Maybe we can create a diversion for the zombies outside for when the stage leaves. Kurt, take the rifles with you. Any other thoughts from anyone?'

Gloria raised a hand. 'Are you sure it says stagecoach? Because there's that canvas covered wagon thing in there. Surely that should be used. It would only need two horses. I mean, what other purpose could it have?'

'We have to follow the instructions,' said Doc. 'Remember those reality TV programmes that used to be on? *Big Brother*? They'll be watching. If we change to the covered wagon, they may punish us in some way.'

Kevin hadn't expected any further questions. 'Right, let's get started. We'll pull the stagecoach out and hitch up the horses.'

'It's not happening today,' said Claudia, adamantly.

'Why not?' asked Prodilyn.

'Those horses have just come off a boat. Who knows where they've come from? They need to be stabled overnight.'

'For the love of God!' continued Prodilyn. 'What are we supposed to do about food in the meantime? The way you're talking, it will be another twenty-four hours before we eat properly.'

'We'll enjoy the biscuits,' said Claudia. 'It's only a day.'

Some people waited in anticipation of the event's first cat fight. The moment passed. Charlie wandered back to the discussion. 'Claudia's right,' he said. 'It can't happen until tomorrow. And we shouldn't go off half-cocked. We should talk through the trip carefully. Otherwise someone could get hurt.'

'Thank you,' said Prodilyn, sarcastically. 'Mr Health and Safety there.'

But people were in agreement. Those keen to get on with things had to defer to common sense. The meeting broke up.

It was coffee and biscuits for lunch. Prodilyn and Gloria refused to eat them in the cookhouse with the others, or with Claudia more precisely, and went to their room.

The horses had been installed in the stables after the coach had been dragged outside. Lee found out then about the zombie snake attack and recounted Frankie King's warning in Chicago.

'I was looking forward to that thing springing out at me,' he said.

'It scared Prodilyn instead,' said Claudia, smirking.

While Claudia and Kurt spent time figuring out how they would go about attaching up the horses in the morning, Lee returned to the bunkhouse. From his luggage he extracted a large, prescription tub of eczema cream. Neither he nor Claudia suffered from the condition (in fact it belonged to a Mr Picchione who had the flat in New Milford before them). Lee squelched his right hand inside the tub and extracted an object sealed in polythene. He wiped it off as best he could with a towel, wiped his hands, then unwrapped the package. Lee loved his original Colt pistol, but here was his Glock 9mm automatic. He had learnt from his experiences in Berkshire not to ever leave himself or Claudia open to the insanity of other people, especially on hair-brained expeditions to Texas. He hid the gun in the one place Claudia would not find it: her own bunk.

In the cookhouse, mid afternoon, Leland was not happy. He had been bumped from the stagecoach mission, in favour of Doc. It was felt the medical practitioner should go along in case of an accident. Of course, Lee was going to accompany Claudia. Kurt sat there, cradling his Winchester; he had volunteered first.

'Why not leave Leila behind?' asked Leland.

'Do you want to tell her?' asked Kevin.

Leland accepted the situation. He still sat there nursing a coffee, listening to the plan. He would be needed in distracting the zombies away from the main entrance. He was to at least have the fun of shooting a few, then he and Andy would throw fireballs of some kind, maybe Molotov cocktails, from the wall just before Devin opened the gate and the stagecoach departed.

Lee knocked on Leila's door. He got no reply. It was late; no one was still up in the cookhouse – some people had gone to bed in a mood, bemoaning the lack of food. He knocked again. Still nothing. He thought about returning along the corridor to Claudia, but by then he felt a little concerned. He turned the door knob slowly and entered the room. Leila looked up at him from a prone position on the lower bunk. She had in earphones, listening to music. She pulled the earphones out and smiled at him.

'Hi,' he said. 'I wondered if you were hungry. We've got these cereal bars.'

She waved him in, and got up to a sitting position. She took two of the offered bars.

'Thanks,' she said. 'Have some crisps, I've brought loads.'

He perused the stash on the top bunk, chose two packets of ready salted. 'Can I take a packet for Claudia?'

'Of course. Does she know you're in my room?'

'Actually, it was her who sent me.'

She laughed. 'Remember when I sent you to her, in the mall?'

'When you'd had enough of me.'

'Used you and discarded you. Sit. Talk to me.'

'So, are you happy not having a room mate? I know sharing with Ruth might have been a bit odd.'

'It's early days. Someone might move in with me.'

Always blunt, he remembered. 'Of course. And why not?'

'I quite like my room,' she said. 'Very minimalist. I looked into your room this afternoon. Bunk beds, as well.'

'I know. I've almost put my back out climbing up there.'

She made a lewd face. 'And the rest.'

'So, Leila, about tomorrow. Claudia didn't just want me to feed you...'

'Did she not?'

'Oh, no. You're going to be taking Kevin's gun. Me and Claudia will be up top, driving. She wanted to make sure you didn't somehow, accidentally, shoot us through the buttocks.'

'I promise to be careful.'

'Good. So, not too freaked out by doing this again?'

'No, not really. Besides, I've got you, Charlie and Jon to watch out for me. And Leland seems nice. Pretty boy Kurt might turn out to be a good friend.'

'Now look who's a popular girl.'

'I'm pleased you're still with Claudia. You and me wouldn't have have worked out.'

'You don't know that. I was well into you.'

'Literally. You know, when I think back to what happened to us, I don't think about the bad stuff. I think of sunbathing on the roof, having that race in the shopping carts, being with you. The nasty stuff – I blank that out.'

'That's probably for the best. Well, I'd better get back before she thinks...'

'Right. See you in the morning.'

He nodded. He wondered about giving her a peck on the cheek or the forehead, did neither and left the room.

FOURTEEN

Kevin found the loudspeaker which was transmitting the crack of dawn reveille bugle call, and shot it. Then he joined the others for breakfast of coffee and biscuits. He sat next to Claudia, who was in the heavy leather coat she had travelled to Chicago in. 'You should be on bacon and eggs this morning.'

'Why's that?' she asked.

'You're going on a mission. Like the RAF in the war.'

She stared at him for a moment, assessing his mental state. 'Right.'

Rather than talk to Kevin, Claudia decided to prepare the horses. She looked to Kurt. The two of them had already been to the stables to check on the animals. 'Shall we, Kurt?'

'For sure,' said Kurt.

As she left with Kurt, Claudia stroked Lee under the chin in passing. 'Ooh, who needs a shave?'

Lee finished his coffee. He was in a similar coat to Claudia. He reached underneath to check his cavalry pistol was in the right position. Then he looked for Leila, who was on the chaise longue talking to Gloria. There was a dusty shaft of light coming through right onto them; it made Gloria seem even more blonde, pale-lipped and downright sexy, and also highlighted the glossiness of Leila's young hair. Leila turned slightly, mid gossip, showing off the cute freckles across the bridge of her nose. Her little cowboy hat was hanging by its string down her back. She suddenly realised he was watching them. "Love the yellow stripe on the leg," she mimed and pointed at him. Gloria just smiled.

Doc came in wearing his black outfit, looking like he hadn't slept very well. He was pale and had three days growth of beard on his chin, but not being very hirsute it tended to congregate around his mouth – if he tried, he could create a superb goatee. He was drinking from a can of lemonade.

'Looks like we've all got little stashes of beverages or snacks,' Lee said to him.

Prodilyn had entered, wearing the sheepskin coat she had purloined at Barbra's ranch. 'Not all of us,' she said to Lee.

She sat down near Gloria. Lee ignored her.

'Are we ready?' asked Doc.

Kevin answered, 'Soon as I've had this coffee, I'll find Leland. We'll be set when you're ready to roll out of this place.'

Doc put his medical bag on the table and sat down for a moment.

'You've got the map?' Doc asked Lee.

'Yep. It's not very complicated.'

'So it just comes down to how good a driver Claudia is.'

'Your guess is as good as mine on that one, my friend.'

'What's the distraction going to be, to move the zombies away?'

Kevin spoke up, 'I smuggled in half a dozen grenades from the former Yugoslavia.'

'Did you?' asked Gloria, astonished.

'No. Miss gullible, you. We're banging pots and pans together.'

'How pathetically small-time,' said Gloria, with high disdain.

'Mount up, troops!' called Claudia from the stagecoach driving seat.

Lee was taken aback by her unusual bravado. All of them, except Prodilyn and Gloria, had come outside to look at the magnificent sight of the four horses harnessed to the gaudy stagecoach.

Lee climbed up alongside Claudia. Kurt, Leila and Doc got into the carriage. Lee looked around him from his lofty position. For the first time he noticed the noose hanging from the gallows, out in front of the jail. He was momentarily shocked by the gruesome sight.

Claudia patted his leg. 'We're off,' she said.

'Take it easy, for God's sake,' he told her.

She took a fresh hold on the reins and then released the brake. Andy signalled to Kevin and Leland, up on the north wall. Leland began firing off his pistol with a dramatic recoil of his right arm. Kevin, his gun belt around Leila's slim hips, had to settle for making a racket with two large saucepans.

After a minute, Devin opened the main gate and Claudia geed up the horses. They moved out slowly. The diversion seemed to have worked in dragging the zombies into a cluster below the noise, but there were three or four stragglers right there, seemingly looking at the stagecoach filling the gateway. Andy stepped through alongside the horses, pistol in hand. He aimed, fired, put a slug through a zombie's brain. He fired twice more, downing two more with amazing accuracy. Lee looked down on the man in passing, then had to hang on as Claudia bumped forward. Andy ran back inside, Devin closed up again.

They had a clear run; Claudia didn't have to trample any zombies after all. A few moved in from both sides, prompting gunfire out of the carriage windows. Still, it was exciting stuff. Lee started to lean over the side to joke with the people inside, until Claudia pulled him back by his collar.

'You'll get your head shot off, you fool!'

He laughed. There came a whoop of delight from Leila below, she must have dropped a zombie, then Lee focussed his attention on Claudia. She was doing so well under extremely abnormal circumstances, going really slowly, but following the train track.

'You're doing great, babe,' he told her. 'When we get home we'll get you a job with a funeral director.'

'You cheeky sod.'

She was grinning, but kept her eyes on the terrain ahead. Lee looked back over the roof of the carriage. The zombies had drifted back around the front again. He couldn't see any heads looking over the walls. Either they were in the front gate blockhouse, or had lost interest now they were clear.

'How we doing?' asked Claudia.

'We're clear. Do you want to stop for a minute? Get your bearings?'

'No, I'm good. Let's push on.'

Lee started to love it. The stagecoach was like the childhood game being played again, the Texas soil being the river – only he'd forgotten to fire his gun during the departure.

Seeming to read his mind, Claudia said, 'You didn't shoot any.'

'No, no. I'm a lover not a fighter.'

It seemed to take forever to cover the distance back to where they had swapped the damaged rail for one from behind the train. Kurt came up to join them for a while, but the weather had turned stormy and the temperature had dropped markedly, so he returned inside. It was raining when they got to the spot where the steamboat captain's map became active. Lee spotted the turn-off and alerted Claudia.

All was quiet, apart from the rain hammering on the roof of the stagecoach and onto Claudia's *Once Upon A Time In The West* hat. There seemed to be no imminent threat from zombie attack – more of a worry was Claudia trying to negotiate the turn on fairly uneven ground, which was becoming slippery. She did it gradually with a lot of encouraging shouts to the horses, and then they were moving along a narrow track lined with boulders.

'I hope we'll be able to turn around,' said Claudia, sounding worried.

'We'll see.'

'We're sliding a lot.'

'Don't lose your nerve now, girl.'

'Thanks for that.'

The rain came across them horizontally. They huddled

together.

'Does this make you homesick for Yorkshire?' he joked.

'Lee, we're getting someplace. Look.'

They could just about make out a building in a clearing up ahead.

'A cabin,' said Lee.

'Thank God we're here.'

Claudia drifted the team wide and came around the front of the cabin so they were facing back out. She stopped the horses and applied the brake. Lee jumped down, to be joined by Kurt and Doc.

'We should watch for an ambush,' warned Kurt, his Winchester at the ready.

Leila got out the other side, aiding Claudia down into the mud. Both girls made a point of stroking each horse in turn. Claudia whispered something into their ears about being back in the stables soon.

Doc was detailed to stay with the girls, as Lee and Kurt checked out the cabin. They went right around the building through the torrential downpour, finding no obvious threat. Back to the front, they saw the only doors were padlocked. Kurt went immediately to blast the lock off with his rifle.

'Steady on!' cried Lee, appalled. 'Try whacking it with the butt first, before you ricochet one of our eyes out.' Kurt did as suggested, but it was never going to give. 'No, you were right. Shoot the fucker off.'

Kurt used his pistol instead. Unlike in the movies it took four shots to damage it enough to be kicked free.

By this time they were all drenched. As they opened the double doors, the last thing Lee and Kurt needed was to be jumped by a couple of zombies. The room was dark but they could make out boxes upon boxes of stores. They all stepped inside to take a respite from the storm. Lee leant in to read what was printed on the nearest box.

'What does it say?' asked Claudia.

'Condoms,' he joked.

She tutted at him.

Doc asked, 'Shall we form a chain, and pass boxes along?'

'Not going to work,' answered Lee. 'My missus has parked too far from the door. Let's just get on with loading.'

So they proceeded to grab boxes of everything and anything a serious apocalypse survivor would have on their list. Kurt concentrated on the bottled water and the long-life milk. They trudged back and forth through the rain and mud. They filled the seats of the stagecoach, and the front and back boots as well. Kurt then climbed up top and they threw things up to him.

No zombie attack came.

'Let's get the fuck out of here,' said Lee.

There was just enough space for Leila inside; Doc and Kurt had to balance on top of the roof supplies. Lee and Claudia retuned to their positions. At first the wheels refused to budge, flooding fear through all of them at the thought of being stranded. But then, under Claudia's spirited encouragement, the horses pulled them clear.

Prodilyn and Gloria were in the bath together (not for the first time since knowing each other). Devin had been good enough to boil the water in the bathhouse and fill the metal tub for them. The girls thanked him, standing there with their towels, soap and bathrobes. He stood his ground.

'Oh, you want me to go now,' he had joked.

'If you wouldn't mind,' said Gloria, smiling.

Devin had grinned and departed. 'I'll tell folks not to disturb you.'

They were top to toe, their hair pinned up. It was debatable whether the cold air temperature was completely overpowered by the hot water. But they weren't complaining, it was wonderfully luxurious in there after the dreadful journey and the austere beginning to the stay in the fort. They'd had a good old chinwag on a number of subjects, mainly about what they missed from the old world – for Gloria it had been her male masseur, for Prodilyn her state-of-the-art wet room, or maybe her Porsche Cayenne.

'I miss Charlie,' remembered Gloria.

'Charlie Higginbottom?'

'No. Charlie. Cocaine.'

They both laughed.

'It's raining,' said Prodilyn. 'I wouldn't want to be out there today. If they don't come back soon I'll scream.'

'What do you want for tea? Steak Dianne? Chicken Biryani?'

'Stop it!'

Gloria laughed even more, causing her breasts to break the soapy surface, and poked the side of Prodilyn's delicate ribcage with her right foot.

'I've just thought of something,' said Prodilyn. 'You remember that scare a few years back, over implants? What if I have some trouble with mine?'

'There are qualified people still about. They just don't

have offices. Oh girl, you could say the same about anything, really. I'm worried about this crown in my back tooth. Where do I find a good dentist?'

'That Doc bloke, what is he?'

'I think he's a proper doctor, not a dentist.'

'Well, he can give me a proper medical soon.'

'Who does he share with? Jon, isn't it? We could double date.'

Doc was soaked to the skin, extremely miserable and hanging on for grim death as the stagecoach rocked and slithered along the trail. Something caught his eye and he drew his gun quickly from under his ribcage. Straining down to see, he realised it must have been a clod of earth collapsing off a bank in the downpour. There was certainly nothing threatening there. It made him think, however, of how speedy he had been on the draw. Was he a natural? His face made something between a grin and a grimace – at least he hadn't fired a shot by accident that time.

As they bumped along beside the track, the horses miserable also, Doc found himself thinking of his wife back in Chicago. His plan had been to keep her out of his head for as long as possible – now there he was feeling melancholic over her right at the start. Perhaps it was the rain, he told himself, and tried to hunker down even more. He looked at Kurt, a black form almost unrecognisable in the torrent of water. Somebody swore, maybe Lee, not out of any alarm, just to register their own unhappiness.

Doc thought of their approach to the fort. If the others were not on the ball then they could have to drive straight into a mass of zombies. If they got stuck, the force of the robots could have them over. His day could get a lot worse.

But the others inside the fort *were* ready for their return – Andy had seen to that, organising the men into keeping watch from the blockhouse above the gate, and it was Jon who spotted the small movement way out there, through the rain. He raised the alarm, Kevin and Leland went back to making a fuss over the north wall, and the body of zombies moved across once more. Devin, the only one bulky enough to open the gate on his own, stood there prepared.

'Getting close!' shouted Jon.

Gunfire intensified from Leland. Those who didn't mind the rain – Andy, Charlie and Michelle – stood in the quagmire of the compound awaiting the stage's return.

'Now, Devin!' called Jon.

Devin opened the gate. The bedraggled horses led the stagecoach slowly in, then Devin closed up again. Steam from the horses' nostrils and from their bodies competed for space with the rain. Claudia applied the brake and sank sideways into Lee's arms.

All the men gathered to receive the boxes tossed off the roof by Doc and Kurt, which they stacked on the cookhouse boardwalk. Leila had no intention of moving any more boxes. She was only interested in looking after the horses. She joined Claudia, waited for her to climb down, then they instinctively hugged.

Doc and Kurt let their fatigued bodies down to the mud. They just about had enough energy to do the high "tennis" handshake.

'We made it,' said Doc.
'Coffee!' suggested Kurt.
Lee watched his two favourite girls in their long embrace.
'Well done, you,' said Leila.
'Thank you,' answered Claudia.
'I think it's a bath for you and the same for me.'
'Jesus!' joked Lee. 'I'll be boiling water all day long.'

FIFTEEN

Leila bathed first that afternoon. When it was Claudia's turn, Lee sat in a Tae kwon-do stretch position on the floor, talking to her. He'd managed to have a wash himself earlier and was thankfully in fresh clothes. He thought his girlfriend made a lovely sight, her legs sticking out over the end of the tub. They both agreed that they were looking forward to doing nothing in the fort for a while. Any more missions could be carried out by the others.

Devin and Michelle were overjoyed to have a full store room, and fed everyone extravagantly that evening. Prodilyn was pleased with the food. Her grumbles moved on to how basic their living conditions were. Some people in the lounge area of the cookhouse listened to her; some didn't. It was gloomy, the kerosene lamps required to be used early on. The rain continued to fall, and it was agreed all round that the mission had finished just in time.

Doc left for bed first, going out with a few pats on the back for his day's efforts. Gloria was tuckered out also, just with the strain of doing exactly nothing. Before she turned in for the night, she perused the bookshelf, reporting to the others, 'They're all bleedin' zombie books.' There was Max Brooks'

World War Z, JE Gurley's *Ice Station Zombie*, and several others, including the complete works of Jonathan Maberry. 'Oh, for the love of God!'

Claudia was sitting there reading on her Kindle. She had no intention of offering it to Gloria.

Lee finished his coffee beside her. He kissed Claudia's cheek. 'Personally, I still like the feel of actually holding a real book in my hands.'

She looked at him, sceptically. 'What was the last book you ever read?'

He had to think. 'That Tae kwon-do manual, last Christmas. No, I tell a lie, there was... no, I'm struggling here, babe. Anyway, I'd prefer to make up stories in my head rather than read from a machine. I've got a great imagination.'

'Have you, now?'

'Oh, aye. Shall we retire for the night and I'll let you know what's in my head?'

She shrugged as if she wasn't particularly fussed, but turned off the Kindle anyway.

Some semblance of routine began to develop in the days following the stagecoach mission. In the warm cookhouse, Charlie and Phil took to playing long games of chess. Those with iPods or MP3 players lounged around in their own worlds, when they weren't chatting with each other. Even Prodilyn, who had gotten off on the wrong foot with most people, engaged in friendly conversations.

Between chess matches, Charlie proved to be the only one who could play the piano (in a fashion). He had to force himself to concentrate intensely on the keys, and the tunes he came out with were slow dirges, almost funereal. His favourites were *The Love Boat, Against All Odds, Run Rabbit Run*. When he started a slow butchery of *The Sound Of Music*, Lee cried out in mock despair, 'What the hell is that shit!?'

Doc had stayed in his room for forty-eight hours, chilled to the bone. Michelle and Leila kept him fed with soup and hot milk, and checked on him regularly. When he did emerge back into the cookhouse, he looked like death warmed up and spoke with a husky voice. He sat himself quietly down near the range cooker, reading VM Zito's *The Return Man*, and coughing every so often.

There was suddenly quite a lot of flirting taking place. None of the women were in costume any more, preferring their jeans or leggings, with long-sleeved tops or hoodies (Leila). So, they were modern girls with no 19th century inhibitions about how to converse with the men.

Prodilyn and Gloria moved effortlessly from Leland to Kurt to Jon. They involved Lee in their chatter whenever Claudia wasn't about. Kevin was not a bad looking man, but his difficult personality stifled any interest in him. Andy kept himself to himself, occasionally glancing over when someone said something to elicit a giggle from the girls. Of course, Devin and the older guys were left out. Also, Doc was currently excluded on health grounds.

Leila moved around the three most eligible bachelors herself. She liked the similarly diffident, reserved personalities of American, Leland and Swede, Kurt. But when she talked with Jon she paid more attention. Everyone could see he was her favourite – discounting the taken Lee, of course.

Some people talked of home – perhaps those who hadn't endured such a traumatic couple of years. Lee noted at one point that Prodilyn talked of friends she would come up and visit in London, as if she didn't live there herself. Perhaps, he wondered, someone had labelled her and Gloria as Londoners out of convenience. He thought no more about it as Charlie mangled *Somewhere Over The Rainbow*.

'He's playing all the right notes,' Jon said to Lee, with a smile, 'but not necessarily in the right order.'

Claudia and Leila had been caring for the horses, checking their hay and water, and mucking them out every day. At the end of the first week the weather finally brightened up. The compound was a quagmire, but they could walk the horses out through the safe west gate and let them wander about on the grass of the bridge approach for a few hours.

Some of the men took to shooting at the wandering zombies for sport. Lee splattered one female head with a shot from a Winchester rifle, and that was enough for him. Immediately, a rivalry sprang up between the teenagers, Leland and Kurt. On the first occasion, Leland came out on top, laughing and taunting Kurt. The Swede took it without comment, but Lee and Jon both noticed that there seemed to be a line that was close to being crossed with the man.

'Perhaps it's a Scandinavian trait,' Jon said to Lee afterwards. 'They are a moody lot. Don't they have the highest suicide rate in Europe?'

'Maybe we should tell Leland not to wind the guy up.'

Night fell quickly over Texas. Lee and Claudia already seemed to be going to bed early and getting up with the sun.

They laughed when he remarked that it was like an old episode of the BBC's comedy *The Good Life*, where the self-sufficiency couple tried to get into a more natural routine and ended up unable to sleep at all.

Leila kept to her regular hours. A couple of times she had coffee with Charlie on the west wall, overlooking the river. The canopy of stars above them was truly awe-inspiring.

'Can you handle all that, Charlie?' she asked, waving an arm over her head. 'It's mind boggling. I watched a documentary once about these pictures of a galaxy taken from the Hubble telescope. It said that the light you saw left that place when the Romans were here on earth – it's that far away.'

'I don't believe it,' he said.

'Believe what? What I just said?'

'Any of it. I'm not particularly religious, but I think all you see is an illusion from God. You think it goes on forever, but it doesn't.'

'Wow, Charlie, that's heavy. But what about the moon? What about Mars? We've sent things to there.'

'Oh well, He stretched to creating Mars. But anything else, you'll just hit the back wall.'

Leila tried to comprehend what he was saying. In the end she just giggled and hugged him. He laughed and cuddled her like a daughter.

'Are you winding me up?' she asked.

'I'm not quite sure.'

They laughed even more.

Leila took another bath. Lee was happy to boil up the water

again and fill the tub. She arranged her soap and shampoo, before removing her hoodie.

'Stay with me,' she said.

'Eh? What? I don't think that's a good idea, Leila.'

'You've watched me bathe before, in the mall.'

'Have I? I don't think I have.' He was edging out. 'I'd better leave you to it.'

Her boots and jeans had come off by this point in the conversation. 'You watched me shower. It's the same thing.'

'*Leila.*'

She was suddenly naked in front of him, her nipples erect in the chilly air, her delicate ribcage stretched up as she piled her hair up on top of her head. Lee almost swore, made himself look away, then looked back. The skin of his ex-girlfriend was as smooth as he remembered, the hips sexily curved, the pubic hair pencil thin.

She stepped into the tub and slid down into the water. 'Hot, hot,' she cried out.

'Do you need some cold?'

'No, I can handle it. Sit. Talk to me.'

'Leila, you're outrageous.'

She started making a lather. 'You're the last person I feel the need to be shy in front of. I love having baths. Will you help me every day?'

'You've got to be kidding?'

'Is it too much like hard work?'

'It's not that, and you know it.'

She laughed. He found a chair and sat down.

'If you don't boil my water, I'm sure one of the other boys will.'

'I'm sure they will. Ask Kurt.'

'I will ask Kurt.'

He realised that he was rocking backwards and forwards as he watched her, so stopped himself.

SIXTEEN

Kurt rammed Leland up against the wall in their room; then Leland spun Kurt around and slammed him up against the wall in turn. Kurt was going for a second try when Leland brought up his knee with great force. Kurt took the pain and launched a head butt, the impact of which Leland mostly managed to avoid. The grappling continued until Andy and Kevin, hearing the kerfuffle, rushed in to separate the pair.

It later transpired that Kurt was a Scandinavian cleanliness freak, while Leland was a grungy American – not the best combination to share a tiny room, in a compound without running water. They were dragged, figuratively speaking, to the cookhouse for a clear-the-air meeting, chaired by Phil, who seemed to be the senior group member present at the time. In front of Andy and Devin, and a fascinated and amused Prodilyn and Gloria, he made both teenagers express what had upset them.

Phil patiently heard them out, before he gave it some thought. He didn't want to ask anybody to swap rooms with one of the boys; that might just spread the problem, so he asked them if they could see their way to compromising. If Leland could be more considerate and Kurt less fussy? They grudgingly agreed and, when prompted by Andy, shook hands.

'Well done, Phil!' squealed Prodilyn, thoroughly entertained. 'You're a born administrator.'

'Thank you, good lady,' answered Phil. 'Whether that's a compliment I'm not sure, but thank you anyway.'

'Hey! Over here!'

The call came from Charlie, checking out storage sheds with Phil behind the jail and the office building. Lee and Jon squelched across as quickly as they could. They arrived as Charlie was extracting a number of lethal-looking archery bows, with quivers full of arrows. At the same time, Phil was finding a collection of shovels.

'Oh, good,' said Jon, grinning. 'We can shoot arrows at the zombies or dig a big hole. Shall we organise a vote on it?'

'Sixteen shovels,' said Phil. 'There are sixteen of us, if you were to count Ruth Rigsby.'

'That is bizarre,' said Lee. 'But forget that. Let's do some archery.'

They climbed up onto the west wall, joined by Leila, Gloria and Devin, who had been smoking a cigarette out the back of the cookhouse.

It was Devin who had the first go, saying he'd done it before in the old days. He positioned an arrow and pulled the string back to his chin.

'I remember the London Olympic archery,' said Gloria to Jon beside her. 'It was held at Lord's cricket ground. There were a few archers with permanent lines on their faces from where the string presses against it.'

'I had something like that when I was a boy. A permanent wound under my chin.'

Devin loosed his first arrow, but lost it into nothing but earth, twenty feet from the nearest zombie.

'What do you mean?' Gloria asked Jon, baffled.

'A snooker scar, from the cue constantly rubbing on my chin.'

She screamed with laughter and hit him on the arm.

Jon grinned, surprised that anyone still did that kind of gesture when highly amused. He noticed Gloria had just the sexiest mouth ever, with perfect white teeth. She took his arm, as Devin tried again.

'Yes!' cried out Leila as the second arrow went into a male zombie's head fifty feet away. It was like one of those joke shop arrows with the band around the back. She stopped laughing when she saw that Gloria had hold of Jon. She cursed herself for not claiming his attention as soon as the game had started.

'I'll have three goes,' said Devin, 'then pass the bow.'

His third arrow seemed to pass straight through a female zombie's leg, but like the male she kept moving about.

Charlie, not one of the gun carriers, tried with another bow, but he wasn't very adept. Leila had a go – her arrows landed threateningly amongst the zombies but without a definitive strike. Gloria encouraged Jon. He took Devin's bow, shakily positioned an arrow and spread his arms. He aimed for a cluster nearby and, after a very long pause that almost started him laughing, he loosed his arrow.

'Yes!' from Gloria, as Jon pierced a zombie's back. She was bouncing on her toes at his side and gave him a congratulatory kiss on the cheek. Leila looked ready to throw a punch at the woman. Charlie noticed this and made Leila come away and have more shots. This time she hit a target and everyone congratulated her.

The fun took up about half an hour. Others would have a go later, but this group decided to come down off the wall and go in for coffee.

'After coffee,' said Jon, 'we'll dig that big hole.'

Gloria laughed again, though she hadn't a clue what he was talking about, and let him help her through the mud.

As soon as they heard about the bows and arrows, Leland and Kevin left the cookhouse to have a go themselves. It was touching how Michelle listened to her husband recounting his efforts. She gave him a kiss, sat him down and went to get him a big piece of apple pie.

Everyone else sat about talking. Doc was there, coughing away, but enjoying his zombie book. Prodilyn sipped coffee, watching over the rim of the mug as Gloria went to work on Jon – the flirting was expertly done, giggling at his jokes, touching his knee at just the right moment. Leila stewed. After a few minutes she got up and went in search of Leland.

Claudia came in and sat on Lee's knee to hear about the archery. As she listened to Jon tell how he hit the zombie in the back, Gloria turned to Charlie in the next seat and congratulated him on his own shooting.

'Thank you,' he answered. 'It was very enjoyable.'

'We've not really had chance to talk, have we, Charlie? You're one of the Blackpool people, aren't you? I'm from Maidstone in Kent myself.'

'Oh, I thought they said London?'

'Close enough, I suppose. I'm quite enjoying this. Are you? It's such a change. I know the world is in such a mess right now, but this is a mess in a no-worries kind of way, isn't it. I'm forgetting all my problems.'

'Lucky you. This place makes me mull over mine.'

'Oh dear, does it? Have you left a wife out there?'

'No, Gloria. I'm no longer married. What about you?'

'What year is it?' She laughed. 'No, not married. Two divorces in my twenties, can you believe? I've got a small family, actually. My life revolves around friends more than family.'

'Brothers and sisters?'

'No, only child. Well, there was a sister, but she died as a baby.'

'I'm sorry to hear that.'

'Maybe that's why I always have a lot of girlfriends around me, to take the place of my sister. Oh, here's me getting all sad when we've had such fun.'

'No, it's right to speak of her whenever you want. Maybe she's somewhere watching you play this silly game.'

'And laughing at me. I do hope so.' She lowered her voice. 'When I was younger I sometimes pretended she hadn't died. That she was around with me.'

'Maybe she was.'

'I beg your pardon?'

'Just a little theory of mine. I'll tell you about it sometime.'

'No, go on, Charlie, tell me now. We've got nothing else to do.'

Charlie settled in his seat. 'I had a daughter, who died

when she was six.' He waved off her gesture of sympathy. 'But then I was annoyed when she got married at seventeen. She then died in a car accident when she was twenty-two. But she also waved me off to this event, with her husband and four kids, and she will outlive me by thirty years.'

He'd lost Gloria straightaway. She sat there staring at him blankly.

'Let me explain,' he said. 'When a child dies, especially a baby, it's the worst of the worst. Nothing comes near to that. But what if, on another level, the child doesn't die, there's no need for grief, for a lifetime of heartache, just the normal joy and normality of a child growing up. Of course, the child might be taken by illness or an accident at a later date, but then another strand of life continues elsewhere. You see him or her off to university, to their own marriage. Of course, the child might lose you or their other parent, or siblings, at some stage, but then again, they don't. What I'm saying, Gloria, is, everyone gets to old age one way or another.'

'My God,' she whispered. 'What an amazing idea.'

'Just a silly theory. I just find it too obscene that a baby can be born, with all the billion chemical miracles it takes to create life, just to die after a few hours.'

'So, somewhere, in another... what you call it, plane, I grew up with my sister, saw her married, have children...'

'Something like that.'

'That's such a nice thing to say. Wow, I'm going to be thinking about that for a long time.'

Prodilyn intervened. Gloria was spending too much time talking to the old man instead of Jon.

SEVENTEEN

That night the fort resembled Sodom and Gomorrah. Devin made love to Michelle, Lee made love to Claudia, Leila made love to Leland, and Gloria made love to Jon, in her bunk, with Prodilyn up above them.

At first, Jon was unnerved by the set up. He had once enjoyed a threesome while at college in London, but never had sex with a woman while another one slept (or lay awake listening) in a bunk a couple of feet above his head. Gloria's smuggled in stash of miniature vodka bottles did loosen him up a little, and then Gloria's sexy mouth did the rest. She went down on him as if they had been isolated in the fort for six months. Jon was out of practice, what with the world going to hell, but it all flooded back to him and he ended up having a brilliant time in the little wooden room. Gloria kicked him out afterwards, and he stood giggling in the cold corridor. Did his immediate expulsion mean that Prodilyn had been awake all along, or was Gloria just like that? He tiptoed to his room. Doc was reading a new zombie book by kerosene lamplight. He just nodded at his room mate's late appearance.

Leila had made the decision to bed Leland while watching

him shoot arrows at zombies, as his expanded chest inside the bowstring had caught her imagination. They rutted like excited youngsters – Leland had rarely spent time with a woman in Chicago, and the ones he knew there were depressed and grim. Leila reminded him of what life should be like – she was vivacious and nubile, sweetly noisy at the right times, and because she had her own room didn't make him leave afterwards.

Somehow they managed to get up early the next morning. Leland trudged through the mud to pump water and boil it for a bath. Leila joined him and they bathed together. By a miracle they were done and dressed when the others started rising to their ablutions. They were first into the cookhouse, where they helped Michelle with the breakfast chores.

A sullen Kurt came in, looked at them, then took coffee back to the bunkhouse.

Prodilyn and Gloria decided to take over the office building, beside the jail. They were bored with lounging about in the cookhouse, so, with Kevin's assistance, they cleaned the place out and made it comfortable enough to spend part of the days in. They received visitors occasionally, and Claudia and Leila would wave to them on their way to care for the horses.

People continued with the jobs that had been assigned to them in the first meeting. It was funny how, in the long Texas autumn days, you could look forward to collecting firewood or doing the washing up after meals. Shooting zombies ceased. Kurt, Andy and Kevin turned their attention to the hand cart on the spur of track. They got it working and managed to ride it down to the main gate and back again several times, sometimes with giggling girls as passengers. It was a great novelty for everyone to see the handle being pumped up and down as if they were in some old silent Hollywood western.

Due to their differing ages, Gloria and Jon were more reserved with each other than Leland and Leila. Leland followed Leila around, helping her with her chores, especially the horses. They never discussed being girlfriend and boyfriend, but it was clearly there. Gloria and Jon reacted normally to each other. Neither made an immediate move to repeat what had happened but it went unspoken that it surely would. At one point Jon smirked to himself, imagining Doc reading on his top bunk as he had Gloria below.

In the end, Leila talked to Jon about it all. One evening, Charlie didn't feel like having a coffee with Leila under the stars, so Jon volunteered. Leila gave Charlie a dirty look in passing, then went outside. She and Jon stood watching the moonlit river rushing by. It was a mild night without any wind. They chatted about nothing of importance, then he told her how much he was enjoying the experience of the Texas fort.

'I'm sure you are,' she sniped.

'Sorry, Leila?'

'Fucking that bitch Gloria.'

'Ah. Is this necessary?'

'What was she like?'

'Can I say ah again? Look at those stars, aren't they amazing?'

'Is she dirty? She looks like butter wouldn't melt, but is she dirty?'

'What do you want me to say?'

'That she's dirty.'

'Okay, she's dirty. It was just sex, Leila. She's not the love of my life. She seems... I was going to say nice. She's all right. She's a woman from England as it is now. By which I mean, not a relationship to really care much about.'

'I still don't know what that means.'

'That I'll go with her. But I don't think there's anything else to it.'

That puzzled her a little and she stayed quiet.

'Anyway,' he said. 'What about you and Leland? What's going on there? He seems to be well into you.'

She drank some coffee, didn't like it, so threw it over the wall, cup and all. Jon did a double-take after it, then another as she relieved him of his own cup, and liked that drink better.

'I only slept with Leland because you slept with Gloria.'

He sighed. There it was again. His little Leila who he had found twice in horrible Blackpool. He took her into an embrace. She threw the second cup over the wall to be able to hold him better.

He laughed. 'Stop that, you litterbug,' he told her. 'What are we going to do with you, Leila?'

'Come to my room.'

He noisily blew out his lips. 'I'm struggling with that. I really want to, but another part of me wants to protect you.'

'Protect me in my room.'

The hug went on for a long time. Finally she realised, for that night at least, he was not taking her up on her offer.

'I'm going to bed,' she told him.

She started to leave him.

'Are we still cool?' he asked.

'Of course.' She swung a leg onto the ladder. 'You know those stars. They're just an illusion put there by God. If you keep going towards them you'll just hit the back wall.'

She disappeared down the ladder, leaving him baffled, looking above him with a slow 360 degree turn.

Cosy on their bunk, Lee and Claudia were musing over events so far.

'It's better than the mall,' she said, fondling the top of his chest. 'It's on a grander scale.'

'They do everything bigger in America, don't you know. What do you think of the people?'

'Not a bad bunch. I'm wary of a couple, though. Andy and Phil.'

'Old man Phil? I understand about Andy, he's well shady, ex-military, I think, but what's bothered you about Phil?'

'I don't know. He just weirds me out.'

'Anyway, we're well into this now. The food could be better, but we're not suffering, are we? Do you miss anything?'

'This may sound daft – I miss the smell of the bakery back home in New Milford. And I miss watching you work-out. You've let yourself slip, you know.'

'It's hard to train in here. I'll try tomorrow.'

'What do you miss?' she asked.

'Nothing. As long as I'm with you I'm cool with everything.' She snuggled in further on hearing that. 'I tell you, though, I'd like to sink some beers watching a DVD.'

'A good western?'

'A war movie. Or a James Bond.'

'When we get out we'll watch all your favourites.'

'Can we really? Does that include *Navy Seals*?'

She cringed under the blankets.

'I know, but it's so good. "If you put it out there, don't be afraid to get it cut off".'

'No, please, don't quote Charlie Sheen at me.'

'"I was insulting your heritage, now we're having dinner".'

'Lee!'

They laughed, then kissed.

As Jon tiptoed along the bunkhouse corridor towards the dulcet coughing tones of his room mate, Doc, he felt terribly guilty. That afternoon, while dropping off firewood to Prodilyn and Gloria's new day retreat, they had offered him coffee and some of Michelle's recently made fruit cake. The conversation, as expected, had quickly turned flirtatious, but it had come from Prodilyn, not Gloria. He found it surreal that he was being focussed on by the other woman. Did he want to play their games, he had to ask himself. The thought of a disapproving Leila filled his conscience, but he didn't come away from them. Instead, he let it build to its climax – making love to Prodilyn, with Gloria in the bunk beneath asleep (or lying awake listening). These two women had provided about the most surreal thing ever to happen to him (robotic zombies aside).

Doc looked up from his book as he entered their room, and again gave him a nod.

EIGHTEEN

Lee seemed to be first up. While Claudia slept, he did some stretches on the floor, then went through a few Tae Kwon-do patterns out on the boardwalk. Devin and Michelle appeared and bid him good morning. They were off to start the fire in the cookhouse. Lee thought the pair to be so conscientious over their role in the compound that they might be plants, placed in there by the organisers – certainly without them, life would have been harsh at the start.

He moved towards the bathhouse, noting that the ground had almost solidified. The sky was red, and the temperature mild. Somebody shouted him. He spun back to stare at the bunkhouse. No one there. Another call came, from outside the west gate. Lee strode across there, seeing part of a man's face through a crack in the timber. The face was high up, so obviously on a horse. Lee didn't converse with the person through the gate, he climbed the ladder and peered over the wall.

'Hello?' Lee called down.

'Morning, there.'

A large tan cowboy hat turned upwards to reveal a face with a goatee beard, looking a little like Buffalo Bill. 'Good morning, there,' the man repeated. His horse was black and white, what Lee would describe as Appalachian.

'What can I do for you?' asked Lee.

'Pony Express, sir. I have a letter for this here fort.'

Fuck me, thought Lee, everyone's an actor. He shook his head. Right, one more unexpected novelty in this thing they were engaged in. 'Give me a minute.'

Lee fetched Devin and together they opened the gate. The rider reached into a leather satchel and produced a letter which he handed to Lee. With that, he touched the brim of his hat, turned his horse and left quickly in the direction of the bridge. Devin locked up again.

In the cookhouse, Michelle served Lee coffee. The letter was on the table in front of him.

'Might as well open it,' said Devin. 'The others can find out in due course.'

Lee opened it, perused it quickly himself, then read it to the other two.

'To find messages from home, follow the track five miles west, on foot. Everyone must go, or no one at all, carrying their own shovel.'

'Is that it?' asked Michelle. 'Honey, that's short and sweet. We have to dig up messages from home?'

Lee shrugged. 'It gets us out for the day, I suppose.'

Everyone digested the contents of the letter in turn as they came in for breakfast. Some, like Prodilyn and Gloria, were thrilled. Others, such as Leila and Phil, wondered who there was out there to be receiving letters from.

When Jon arrived, Prodilyn told him the news and showed him the letter, entering into his personal space with a hand resting on his right hip. Leila still thought Gloria was Jon's dish of the day, so the closeness between the two came as a shock to her. It was made worse when she realised she had let Gloria see her unhappiness.

'What can we do?' whispered Gloria, 'he's a popular boy.'

It was the first sign of a bitchy side to Gloria, a person with an agenda, apparently. But the moment was swamped by new arrivals to the cookhouse becoming excited with the mission, so Leila had to let it pass.

Claudia entered and sat on Lee's knee. 'What's all the fuss?'

'We're going on an expedition, to pick up letters from home.'

'Oh, God, really? Who do you think we've got?'

'Well, in my thinking I'm down to Auntie Susan in Chester. You?'

'No idea.'

Leila had moved away for coffee.

Gloria followed the younger woman. 'It was so funny,' she informed her, 'I had him while Prodilyn slept above us. Then Prodilyn had him while I slept below. Although I didn't manage to sleep much. You can imagine how disturbing the sight is of a bouncing mattress in front of your face.'

'Are you looking to have your teeth knocked out?' asked Leila.

'Well! What's rattled your cage? Anyone would think he was your boyfriend, or something.'

'Just leave me alone.'

'Glad to, love!'

Damage done, Gloria moved away, immediately engaging

Kevin in friendly conversation about where they were to be going and who could possibly be writing to them. His wife, he told her, he was sure of it.

Fifteen shovels were distributed – Ruth's was left behind. Michelle and Devin passed out water bottles, then they trudged off in the early afternoon, over the bridge for the first time.

'Not a patch on the Housatonic river,' Claudia said to Lee, as they looked over the edge.

Leland and Kurt went ahead with the Winchesters, Andy lingered in the rear. It was a cross between a gold-mining expedition and a church walk.

Leila strolled arm in arm with Charlie. Jon walked between Prodilyn and Gloria, making sure not to touch either. Lee and Claudia found Kevin beside them with enough conversation to take up a few of the five miles. Devin and Michelle struggled with the exercise, as did the unwell Doc, all falling to the back with Andy.

Like Kevin, Doc was desperate to hear from his wife. Even if not all of them had to go, he would have been along. His shovel was over his right shoulder. He tried not to think of the long walk, or the sun when it got under his hat. Michelle and Devin kept encouraging him and he was grateful to them.

They stayed alongside the track, passing a red barn and a wood in full autumn colours. Then the land fell away to their left and they could see for miles across the beautiful Texas landscape. The group was quite spread out by then. Those at the front decided to stop for a rest, so everyone concertinaed up and found places to sit and drink their water. Jon found himself in a little group with Prodilyn, Gloria and Phil, but he was facing Leila. She was sitting in an unladylike fashion with the knees of her jeans spread, leaning forward. He realised that he could look straight down her top. It wasn't the first time he had been presented with that image – when he was buying her a meal during the first time he had found her, there was wonderful cleavage on show that time. He suddenly realised, despite the sexy, model-like forms and liberated attitudes of Prodilyn and Gloria, he really wanted to spend his time in the fort with Leila. She was gorgeous and cute, and he had been a fool to stick to some outdated idea of chivalry just because he knew her life had been troubled and that she had been only sixteen when he first encountered her. Once they were back from that particular mission he intended to win her over. It may prove hard, he thought, the way she just raised her head and looked daggers at Prodilyn.

'Let's move on,' said Doc.

'Are you sure?' asked Gloria. 'Wouldn't you like to rest some more?'

'I'm not coughing, so we should make hay.'

'Sounds a good idea,' said Andy, the only one who hadn't sat down.

It was tough to get going again. Lee had to haul Claudia to her feet.

'Come on, Grumpy,' he said to her.

'All right, Dopey.'

'Hi Ho.'

Leland and Kurt took point again, while not actually talking to each other. The group followed the railway track as it bent off into more wooded country. It wasn't more than an hour before Leland raised his arm in the military way to stop them. They all piled in alongside him.

'What is it?' asked Prodilyn. 'I'm all done in. It'd better be our location.'

'Oh, my Lord, look at that,' said Michelle.

To the left of the track stood a graveyard, encompassed by black cast iron railings. It had been made to look old, with headstones at all angles and shrubs growing in between. They all began to approach apprehensively. Andy was first into the graveyard. There was no obvious threat so he holstered his pistol. He gestured for Kurt to take a look at the nearest gravestone.

Kurt leant in, reading, 'Here lies Kurt Gustafson. Born Gothenburg, June 20th 1999, died Texas, October 2018.'

'Oh dear,' said Michelle.

Lee had found his grave, alongside Claudia's. Claudia was less than impressed. They all stepped about looking for their graves. Gloria found hers and immediately burst into tears.

'What the hell is this?' asked Leland.

Doc just coughed over his grave.

'This is a nasty joke,' said Charlie.

'Fucking hell!' shouted Kevin, causing everyone to spin round to look at him, but he was only making a point. 'These buggers want us to dig in our own graves for letters from home. Can you believe that?'

The sun left them, covered by heavy cloud. There was no threat of rain, yet it became cool and grim in the graveyard.

'Everyone,' called out Andy, surprising them. 'No need to be upset. Just get in there and find what you want. It's only soil.'

'Good ol' Texas soil,' joked Kevin.

Jon started digging. 'What the hell, I'm getting on with it.' He was alongside Prodilyn. He indicated her headstone. 'Have you been lying about your age, Prodilyn?'

'You cheeky sod.'

Everyone broke ground. Some were quick, some found it extremely distasteful. Gloria suddenly screamed again (she was good at that sort of thing) and scared people out of their minds.

'What's wrong with you?' demanded Leila.

Gloria was pointing down into her grave. At the same time, Kevin and Andy made similar discoveries, and by then there was an overpowering stench of death about them all.

'Oh, for the love of all things holy!' cried out Kevin.

Beneath his spade he had unearthed a putrid, stinking zombie corpse. So had Andy. Gloria turned away from her grave into Jon's arms. Lee had got down on to his fetid cadaver with his spade. Claudia stopped short when she realised what was happening.

'Fuck it,' said Leland, dragging the corpse out of his grave, before continuing to look for his prize.

Kurt pushed on too and, through a coughing fit, so did Doc. Devin got his hands under his corpse, rooting around for any package. Michelle, although feeling nauseous, wanted her correspondence so badly that she copied her husband.

It was gruesome, disgusting, stinking work that only half of them could face. And all the time it was happening, a great mass of zombies had been encroaching on them along the track. Gloria finally saw them when they were twenty yards away – cue scream! Leland reacted first to reach for his

Winchester and pop off a few rounds. Kurt joined him.

'Out!' shouted Jon. 'Everyone out!'

A scramble ensued, Kevin, Andy and Lee firing off their Colts, Devin guiding the women out of the graveyard, followed by the older men. Claudia still had her shovel, swinging it to smash in the face of the nearest zombie, fake blood and brain matter splattering all over her. Lee shot the next one in the forehead and it collapsed, and then he used his body to force Claudia to back away. Amid the chaos he found he could look for Leila, who was copying Claudia with a swinging shovel.

Jon pulled the arms of the females near to him, Prodilyn and a near-hysterical Gloria, then he moved for Leila. Noise of firing and gun smoke all around. He got to Leila but she was down, her legs being mauled. He fired twice into the back of the rabid zombie that had the girl on the floor, then his gun was empty so he smashed the back of its head in with the weapon.

The group was scrambling away from the graveyard, bodies of zombies in their wake. Doc went back to help Jon, as did Lee, and they got Leila clear and dragged her down the track. Leland and Kurt kept picking off zombies as the group retraced their steps. Finally they were out of ammunition, so ran to catch up with the rest.

Now zombies came from the side. Claudia did two with her spade, adding to the detritus on her face. Kevin managed to reload his pistol before he had to fire again. Charlie, unarmed, defied his age to kick a zombie away into shrubbery.

'Keep going!' shouted Andy.

Finally they seemed to be clear, able to slow their flight to a panting walk.

'Damn!' shouted Andy, seeming to blame himself for not posting guards at the cemetery. 'Is everyone with us?'

A quick look around showed they were all there. Doc checked Leila's legs. He had not brought his medical bag with him, but promised to see to her as soon as they were back in the fort. The hike back continued, pausing only at the site where they had stopped on the way out, to finish their water and catch their breath. Some of the men checked their weapons.

'I'm completely out of bullets,' Lee said to Jon.

'Me too.'

'Leila?' asked Lee, 'Are you all right?'

She shrugged. 'It's like what happened to you in the mall. Only worse, of course.'

Those listening nearby took notice of that comment. They all knew the event had taken place before, but the three participants had not spoken of it, and they had not pushed for information.

Prodilyn said to Lee, 'You were very brave to go back for Leila.'

Claudia had to stand there and listen to the compliment for her boyfriend rushing to the aid of another woman. But there was the bond of the shopping mall between them, so she went to be at Leila's side for the final leg back to the fort.

The air temperature was cold, but exerting themselves in direct sunlight had left them a desperate, exhausted lot as they crossed back over the river. Devin came from the rear to get them back into the fort. They all went in search of water, before crashing out in and around the cookhouse.

'That was horrendous,' said Devin, to no one in particular.

Doc tried to control his coughing, while Gloria sat with her dusty face in her hands. Lee tried to wipe some of the mess from Claudia's face. After a few minutes she headed to the bathhouse, waving to Lee that she would be fine alone while she cleaned up a bit. Michelle went too. Then Leila headed that way.

'Leila, I need to see your legs,' called Doc.

Kevin managed a light cheer at that.

'I'll come and see you in a moment, Doc,' Leila told him. 'I've got to go pee.'

Lee smiled through his fatigue at the sight of Leila hobbling away. Lovely Leila.

NINETEEN

It took a good few hours to get over the zombie attack. Leila's wounds turned out to be superficial and were bandaged up by Doc. She sat there with her legs across Leland's thighs. Everyone had washed themselves in turn and had something to eat. As they all discovered in the cookhouse, late afternoon, only eight of the fifteen people came away from the cemetery with an envelope. Devin and Michelle were rewarded for getting down and dirty with their hands, with letters from their respective mothers. Doc sat quietly reading a message from his wife, as did Kevin. Leland had a letter from his sister in Minnesota, but Kurt had been unable to find his, something which drove another wedge between the two men. Gloria and Andy read letters but didn't explain who they were from. Lee had the last one, not from his guess of Auntie Susan in Chester, but from his real, estranged father, who he had not seen for five or six years. In fact, he had taken the surname of his stepfather in 2012, a man who had died in the rioting with Lee's mother.

Lee was too shocked to read it at first, just letting Claudia know who it was from. 'We'll look at it later,' he told her, 'in our room.'

She had nodded and held his hand. Neither of them had expected anything as bizarre as that. When the chaise longue became free, Lee decided to get the letter out of the way. He led Claudia over there by the hand and she sat with her feet underneath her while he read what his father had to say.

'Nothing exciting,' Lee told her. 'Never is with him. Apparently he's in some place called Olyphant in Pennsylvania, with an American woman. What's that all about, I wonder? Claudia, how did these people find my father? What's going on here, babe? I mean, we thought the shopping mall thing was big, but this is epic. This is off the scale.'

'What does your father say?'

'Just wishes us good luck. Hopes to see us at the end of it all. He can whistle for that meeting. Claudia, I'm sorry you didn't find your letter.'

'It's all right. Don't worry about it.'

They snuggled up together.

Phil seemed the most disturbed by the graveyard incident. The fact that he couldn't think who could possibly be writing to him had upset him greatly. He sat silently at the piano, watching all the chat and the swapping of some of the letters.

Some of the men took an inventory on the ammunition. It went from low to nonexistent in Lee's case. The Winchesters were down to ten rounds between two rifles. Andy suggested a ban on all non-emergency firing, and received nods all round.

'Hopefully we can stay inside now,' said Jon. 'Put our feet up for a while.'

Leila dug her heels into Leland's thighs as she gave Jon her best dirty look. Jon hadn't even been thinking of Leila, and tried to express that sentiment with his expression to her, but she had looked away.

'Leland, will you help me to my room?' Leila asked.

Leland got to his feet and scooped Leila up into his arms.

'Help, she said, not carry,' murmured Kurt.

'Stow it, mack,' said Leland from the side of his mouth as he carried Leila out.

Prodilyn and Gloria took coffee and retired to their day room. Not long after, Charlie decided to take some air. He wanted to see if the cemetery zombies had closed in on them, making them effectively surrounded. Jon decided to go with him. They climbed up the ladder, pleased to immediately see the bridge and its approaches completely clear.

'How are you doing, Charlie? Personally, I'm shattered.'

'I'm not too bad. I'll hurt tomorrow. Beautiful part of the world, isn't it?'

'It certainly is.' Jon leant on the wall, watching the river. 'Being in this place makes me feel like I'm in a war. Long bouts of doing nothing, interspersed with frantic action.'

'You did well rescuing Leila.'

Jon joked, 'Not a word of thanks from her.'

'She's pissed off with you. Isn't that the phrase? What do you expect? It's obvious she wants to be with you.'

'I've seen the light, Charlie, believe me. I just need to get the time with her to convince her. She has a bit of a temper, in case you haven't noticed.'

'Best stay away from those two silly cows while you're waiting. There's something not right about them.'

'In what way? I know they're a bit up themselves, but what London woman isn't?'

Charlie lifted a hand. 'Just mark my words.'

'Gloria told me what you said to her the other day.'

'What did I say to her? I talk a lot of nonsense in my old age.'

'About life continuing on a different plane, following a tragedy. I thought that was wonderful.'

Charlie nodded his thanks.

'I'll put in a good word with Leila,' Charlie said, 'if you want.'

'Please do.'

'Look, there's our boy Leland,' said Charlie. They watched Leland walking back to the cookhouse. 'He didn't stay very long. Why not go and see how she is?'

'I'll do that, Charlie. Good talking with you.'

Jon descended the ladder and headed into the bunkhouse. He found Leila not at home. He puzzled for a moment, thought she might be at the latrines, and sat on the lower bunk to wait.

Leila had made Leland change route – she felt she deserved a proper bath again after all her trials and tribulations. She had him boil up water and fill the tub, then peremptorily excused him.

Surprised at how politely he left, Leila stripped quickly in the cool air. As she bent to check the water temperature, someone took away part of the light near the doorway.

'Oh, sorry,' said Lee. 'My timing's not deliberate.'

'No worries. Your regular chair is over there.'

'I'll leave you to it.'

'Lee. Don't be silly.'

He sat down, actually quite tired. Leila was trying to get into the bath without using her bandaged feet, but was not strong enough. It was quite comical to watch, really.

'A little help here, please,' she asked.

He rushed to assist her, picking her up without any effort and lowering her into the water, with her feet dangling over the end of the tub. He didn't return to the chair, just squatted there, needing to be near to her.

She splashed her chest, sighed, then pretended to find him there. 'Oh, hello.'

'You make quite a picture,' he told her.

'It's the light in here. Works wonders for me.'

'Fancy getting caught by a zombie, Leila. We're supposed to be the experienced ones.'

'Yes, very traumatic. Look at my bandages, aren't they neat?' She handed him a bar of soap. 'I don't think I'm up to washing myself.'

'Is that so?' He made a lather. 'I'll start you off, then I'm getting out of here.'

He focussed on her flatter than flat stomach and her particularly tight belly button.

Outside the bathhouse that exact moment, a brief conversation was taking place.

'Looking for Lee?' asked Gloria.

'I am,' answered Claudia.

'I think you'll find him in there.'

'Well, thanks, but that was where I was going, anyway.'

Claudia stepped into the dark bathhouse and stopped dead. If it wasn't so awful, it would have been amusing – Leila in the tub with her bandaged feet sticking out towards

Claudia, the girl's face surprised, while Lee was caught with his fingers in the cookie jar, his expression one of guilty resignation.

Lee caught up with Claudia halfway between the bathhouse and the bunkhouse.

'What the hell was that!?' she demanded to know, spinning on him as he tried to take her arm. 'Do you think because we're doing this nonsense again you can have both of us?'

'Babe, I wasn't thinking at all.'

She burst out crying, not something he was used to seeing from her. She broke free and entered the bunkhouse.

'Where are you going?' he asked, chasing after her.

'Throwing you out!'

'Claudia, where am I supposed to go? Come on, don't be silly. Don't you think you're overreacting?'

They had made it to their room by then, with her immediately throwing his possessions towards the door.

'Claudia,' he appealed, between dodging his deodorant can. 'I bumped into her there.'

'Just like old times, was it?'

'We got talking. It's no excuse. I just forgot myself.'

'No, Lee, you forgot me.'

She suddenly stopped what she was doing and stood stock still. 'Please just go away. I can't stand to be near you just right now.'

Lee could not remember ever arguing with Claudia before, especially with their needing each other so much through the recent hard times. The fury in her eyes advised him to step out of the room, to let her cool down, work it out later. Even still, standing there in the corridor, he tried to think where he would sleep that night, assuming she dragged things out that far. Ironically, the only spare bunk was in Leila's room.

Lee wasn't homeless for long. Kurt and Leland came to blows, probably over Leland's constant reading of his letter from home, and Kurt flounced out (if such a thing was possible from the expressionless Scandinavian). The Swede took Ruth's mattress and bedding and set himself up in the covered wagon in the stables. Being a bit of a clean freak, he scrubbed the inside first, and then spread blankets across all the surfaces. At first it provoked surprise and discussion amongst the others in the cookhouse, but then it seemed as good a place as any to bed down. Perhaps, someone suggested, he had been planning to go there for a while, anyway.

Leland was fine with having Lee join him, for one night at least. He offered his guest assurances that all would be back to normal with him and Claudia in the morning.

But all wasn't well in the morning, as Claudia proved steadfast in her refusal to have anything to do with Lee. The incident quickly became common knowledge, and it was equally obvious that such a festering problem would imprint on all of them in such a confined space.

None of the three parties involved could avoid each other. There was no attempt to communicate or, on Lee and Claudia's parts, to attempt any sort of reconciliation. Leila felt slightly guilty, but as she believed there had been no attempt to steal Lee away from Claudia, she offered no apologies.

It might have been a good time for a mission to occupy all their minds, but nothing transpired – days dragged by with the bad atmosphere lingering over the camp. Jon did encourage Lee to make amends, but Lee was a little shocked really. He was no stranger to fighting with and making up with girlfriends, but not with Claudia. It was all supposed to be different with her.

Claudia bubbled with fury, both at herself for taking it beyond the point of no return and at Lee for his own stubbornness and gross stupidity in the first place.

Life slowly continued in the fort, running alongside the estranged couple. Jon finally found the time to express his feelings to Leila, who took the information coolly. Inside she was giddy with happiness, but there was no rush, she would let Jon suffer a little longer for his mistakes with the London women.

Prodilyn and Gloria paid a visit to Kurt in his covered wagon, taking along coffee and some of Michelle's freshly baked cakes. He had it quite snug in there. They all sat talking, like children playing a game, with the nearby sounds and smells of the horses.

Caring for the horses provided the bizarre reason for Claudia and Leila to interact. They had never really been friends anyway, just two girls thrown together in unusual circumstances, so they just got on with mucking out and exercising the horses near the bridge. Because of the graveyard incident, Leland volunteered to stand guard whenever the girls went outside the fort.

The horses were usually dealt with early in the day, so

Kurt was around to engage the two girls in conversation, sometimes leaning out of his wagon in just his shorts. Once again, his handsome appearance outweighed his dour Scandinavian character.

'Would you?' Leila asked Claudia one morning, indicating the topless Swede climbing down from the wagon to step into his boots and have a big yawn and stretch.

Claudia didn't know if Leila had forgotten Lee or not. 'I don't think so,' she answered. 'You?'

'Me? No.'

'Someone else, perhaps?'

'I never need a fella, Claudia.'

'Not even Leland?'

'Leland's cute. I think I might give in to Jon, sooner or later.'

The girls led the horses out through the west gate. Leland wandered after them and sat himself down on a rock. The horses took their usual interest in the thick grass.

'I've just remembered,' said Leila, 'I went to school with a girl called Karen Goodpasture.'

Leland laughed. 'That's the best surname I've ever heard.'

'Claudia, when do we have to give the horses back?'

'I think the boat is due back next week,' answered Claudia.

As Claudia spoke, she was looking at storm clouds on the horizon, with a flash of lightning within the darkness.

'A storm's coming,' said Leland.

'We've got at least half an hour,' said Claudia.

Inside the fort, Charlie was on the west wall, himself monitoring the approaching storm, as well as watching the youngsters with the horses. Suddenly he turned and shouted down to Kurt, who was moving about carrying the Winchester as a toy. 'Kurt, I need the rifle, now!'

Kurt threw the Winchester up without question. Charlie cocked the weapon and raised the butt to his shoulder. A rogue zombie was shuffling towards Claudia and Leila. Charlie took his time, focussing, while in his peripheral vision he knew Claudia had turned and recognised the threat, he pulled the trigger, and the back of the zombie's head exploded. The report of the rifle shot brought everyone rushing outside, and they gathered with Claudia, Leila and Leland in the gateway. Charlie came down the ladder to have Leila throw her arms around his neck.

'Well done, Charlie, boy,' said Kevin.

'Yes, some shot,' said Devin.

Claudia thanked Charlie with just a shared look. Lee tried to check on Claudia's well-being, but she rebuffed him, wanting to return to the horses. Andy and Kurt went outside to provide security – Leland being sacked from that position.

Charlie wanted no hero fuss over his actions, retiring to the cookhouse for a coffee, where Jon joined him, turning a chair back to front to sit astride it and look at the man.

'Go on,' teased Jon.

'Go on what?'

'Where did that shot come from? That was the work of a marksman.'

Charlie drank his coffee. 'I was sixteen years with the Merseyside Police Firearms Unit.'

'An ex-rozzer. That's brilliant. I knew there was something about you when I first met you in Blackpool.'

'Jon, I'd appreciate it if you kept what I've just said to

yourself. I just want a quiet time in here.'
'Charlie, my lips are sealed.'

TWENTY

There was nothing to do but watch the storm. If Kurt were to describe it, he would no doubt say "that's the wildest storm I've ever seen in my life". Someone in the cookhouse suggested it might be normal for Texas. Lee stood on the bunkhouse boardwalk with Jon, watching the lightning flash every few seconds through the torrential rain. He could no longer see her, but he knew Claudia was outside the cookhouse talking with Leila. How ridiculous, he felt, that he had fallen out with his girlfriend over Leila and yet the two girls had carried on as before. They were only about a month in; he knew they would make it up, and it would be wonderful to do so, yet right then he felt miserable and cold – which doubly upset him, because electrical storms usually delighted him and made him high.

'That's enough for me,' he said to Jon and went to his bunk in Leland's room. Leland was absent. Lee was in possession of a zombie novel from the library. He picked it up for a moment before deciding against it.

He lay down and listened to the rain on the roof, and then the clash of thunder. His mind drifted back to growing up in Cheshire, when global warming was the in thing, and seemed to remember most summers being wet and stormy. Certainly, when he was hanging out with his first real girlfriend in the summer of 2016, a certain hyperactive blonde called Joanna, the bad weather was a good excuse for constant sexual activity.

Beyond Joanna (running through his short list of lovers as it currently stood at the age of twenty-two) he remembered hotel workers, Olivia and Mandy: Mandy in particular who was incredibly thick, accepting the position of chambermaid without understanding the first aspect of what that role entailed. But she was so very sexy, and much more adventurous than Olivia. Then there had been Francesca in Manchester, a brief, passionate fling, staying with her in her daddy's penthouse apartment in the flash Beetham Tower in the city centre. Then realising they had absolutely nothing in common and, in fact, possibly didn't even like each other very much. Again, fantastic sex, but he had to get out of there. He went to stay with a friend in Liverpool, in a flat with a view of the Liver Buildings. Liverpool to him had meant Rachel Rimmer, his last girlfriend before signing up for the shopping mall madness. Rachel, the only ex he knew for sure to no longer be alive, had been brilliant. Lying there on his bunk he had to smile to himself; Rachel had been a go-getting sort of girl, moving him into a flat in Anfield with her while they worked at McDonalds and she got her degree. Beautiful, flame-haired Rachel, with an incredible body and dirty mind: the one who had encouraged him to sign up to the thing. How different life would now be if she had come along too, as initially asked? He would probably not have become friends with Leila in Berkshire, or moved on to Claudia, certainly not moved to be near Claudia's relatives in New Milford, Connecticut.

Claudia. That moody Yorkshire lass. As beautiful as any of them, more special than all of them. The love of his life. Leland chose that moment to enter the room and shake rainwater all over the floor. Lee just looked up at him.

'It's Biblical out there, man,' said Leland. 'What are you doing?'

'Hunkering down.'

'I'm after dry socks, then I'll leave you to it.'

Lee watched Leland change his footwear and then leave with an "adiós", before returning his thoughts to Claudia. He would sort things out, make things better, as soon as possible. She was his woman and it was ludicrous that they should be apart in that way. He would not take any more moodiness from her, he would go out and find her, and bring her back to their room. Just as soon as the rain stopped.

If Claudia were to reminisce about her previous lovers, which were almost double Lee's total, one thread would run right through them; they were all blond lads, from fifteen-year-old best friend, Thomas, at home in York, via several boys at university, to Doctor Plummer at the surgery where she worked before going to Berkshire. All blond except Lee. Maybe just once, she joked with herself about there being little choice in that shopping mall. But, no, she clicked just right with Lee. She felt safe and loved and always kept interested. Perhaps that helped explain the mystery of her current stubborn behaviour, her refusal to get beyond the silly little scene in the bathhouse.

She was in the stables, having run there through the storm because she hated the thought of the horses being frightened by the thunder. She had completely forgotten it was also Kurt's home, and was surprised when he popped his blond head through the canvas opening in his wagon.

'I've been talking to them,' he said.

'So that's why they're trembling.'

'Excuse me?'

'Never mind. Go back to whatever you were doing.'

'I was drinking cocoa given to me by Devin. It's very nice, would you like some?'

Claudia laughed, as she continued moving between the horses to stroke their necks. 'No, you're all right, thank you.'

'Your head's all wet from the rain. I've got a towel, come in.'

'What, into your love wagon? I'm surprised you've not got Gloria in there. Or Prodilyn.'

Kurt's usually deadpan face did crinkle a little around the eyes. 'Suit yourself.'

He withdrew his head. Claudia felt stupid. She went over and looked inside the wagon, lit by a kerosene lamp. 'I would like some cocoa, actually, Kurt.'

He helped her climb inside and she found herself sitting on cushions he had pilfered from the cookhouse. He threw a towel onto her lap and she dried her hair while he poured out some cocoa.

She looked about her at the curved canvas roof, then accepted her mug of cocoa.

'I've not had cocoa for years,' she said.

She had to lift her hands out of the way as he squeezed

past her, but he was only closing the flap. He settled down closer than before. Claudia noted this fact, but kept sipping her cocoa.

'What do you think of my home?' he asked.

'It's fun. I wish I'd thought of it first.'

'For when you were a couple, or now?'

She ignored the question. 'Don't you get cold in here?'

'I'm from Sweden. What's cold about the USA?'

'Well, maybe it didn't bother you, but I've been freezing in Connecticut.'

'Anyway, it gets warm in here, with body heat.'

'I bet it does.'

She put down her cup, and when she came back up he was there beside her – definitely more cheeky than creepy, obviously he was good at making moves.

'So, Claudia, what's happening? Are you and Lee finished? Yes? He's a nice man, but I'm pleased if it's true.'

Up close and personal she found him extremely pretty, his teeth were wonderful for a European, and that blond hair turned her on something chronic. He seemed to take her silence for a green light to try for a kiss. She stopped him with a hand to the chest – a hand that stayed on the chest.

'Easy, tiger,' she said.

He pushed on – she laughed.

'Sorry,' she said. 'For a moment there I thought I was in the Winnebago of a boy band member.'

That completely baffled him, amusing her even more. He was so cute, she felt. Suddenly there was kissing. They were both intense – he because that was the way he behaved with women, she because it felt so wrong, such a betrayal of Lee.

Kurt's hand was on the left side of her panting ribcage. It needed to be on her breast, so she put it there. Tongues were shared. She loved blond guys. He started to undress.

'Hey, hold on, kiddo,' she said.

'What?'

'Hold your horses. I'm just not ready... you know.'

'What's wrong, Claudia?' He tried to continue. She headed out of the wagon. 'Claudia?'

'Thanks, Kurt. You're really cute, but I'm not that interested.'

She blew kisses to the horses on the way out.

'Your loss!' called Kurt.

'I'll live with it!'

Claudia ran out into the storm, wanting to go to Lee, but finding herself headed to the cookhouse instead.

Phil sat in the jail, wearing his NY Mets baseball cap low, watching through the window at the rain dripping from the hangman's noose. He was cooked already; his first month felt like a year. He possessed no patience whatsoever, had no tolerance for the foibles of the general public – fourteen of whom he had allowed himself to be locked up with. Back in New Milford he despised the moronic people he had to serve in the coffee shop, that job which necessity had forced him to lower himself to. He had been a man of standing in the county, before all the trouble, and to then have to wait on people who had once been his peers, and even worse, on people who he had once looked down upon. Life was grim, and getting grimmer in the wilds of Texas.

In a completely different mindset, Devin and Michelle sat

watching the rain outside the back of the cookhouse. They were still loving the experience, still together, cooking, being with different kinds of people. Devin remembered watching the Bears beat the Texans at Soldier Field, and Michelle was fairly obsessed with the Kennedy assassination, so Texas worked for them both.

Inside the cookhouse, Jon played Charlie at chess; Doc was playing cards with Kevin. Andy had forced himself to start a zombie book. Gloria was trying to bring some femininity to Leila's nails, while Prodilyn snoozed in the armchair. All in all, they were somewhere between how Phil and Devin and Michelle felt.

Claudia and Lee arrived simultaneously at the door. She shook herself free of rainwater on the boardwalk, while he politely stepped back to let her go in first. She didn't exactly blank him, but without a word went in search of coffee.

'I've just checked the river,' said Lee, to everyone. 'It's almost over the top of its banks. If it stays like that I can't see the boat coming back this week.'

Thinking of the horses, Claudia flashed a look at Lee, then went back to the coffee pot on the stove.

GB Hope

TWENTY-ONE

'*Dinnerladies*,' said Gloria to Kurt, in his wagon, later that day, 'by Victoria Wood. Brilliant comedy show.'

'I don't know it.'

The storm still raged around their part of Texas. Dared on by Prodilyn in their day shack, Gloria had sploshed through the mud to attempt a seduction of Kurt. He was a sure thing. They lay in his bed between copulations, and for some reason she wanted to educate him on the subject of British television comedy shows.

'*Porridge*,' she flung at him.

'Breakfast food?'

'*Porridge*, with Ronnie Barker. You must know that one? The prison one. "It's a plant. No, it's not, it's a tin of pineapples".'

'Gloria, I'm worried for you.'

She laughed. '*Only Fools and Horses.*'

'Yes! I've heard of that. David Jason. "Rodney, you plonker!".'

Gloria screamed with delight. 'You adorable Swedish man, you.'

Lee was standing at Charlie's shoulder as Edward Elgar's *Land of Hope and Glory* was being murdered on the piano. Claudia strode the length of the cookhouse to throw herself into Lee's arms.

'I'm so sorry,' she said. 'Lee, I'm so sorry.'

'No, no, no, it's me who should be saying sorry. I've been such an idiot.'

Emotion flowed through both of them as they stood there for a long time. Some people in the cookhouse had noticed, and some hadn't. Lee kissed Claudia and wiped away her tears.

'Friends again?' she asked.

'You are so beautiful.'

A loud thunderclap sounded immediately above them, causing Claudia to whimper and burrow her face into his chest.

'Silly weather,' she said.

'I told you, everything's bigger in the US.'

'Lee, I've missed you. Let's not fall out again, please.'

'I promise. Come on, let's sit down somewhere.'

'No, Lee. Take me to bed or lose me forever.'

Charlie had continued to play while the love affair was being rekindled at his back. He came to what he thought was the end and looked over his shoulder, asking, 'Have you any requests?'

Both Lee and Claudia smiled at him. Lee patted his shoulder and shook his head. He took Claudia's hand and led her to the bunkhouse.

Foreplay carried out beneath the loudest thunderstorm in the history of the world provoked several unintentional sniggers, from both Jon and Leila. Once she cried out, making him laugh. But it was still a wonderful, leisurely time which they had waited so long for.

He slipped down her naked body to use his mouth, tenderly and sparingly, incorporating her inner thighs and those delicious areas just inside the hip bones. Overcoming her pleasure, to escape the thunder, she moved down to be with him, finding his face to kiss under the covers. She sucked his tongue into her mouth and reached down to cup his balls, something she had once been told to do by a boyfriend in Blackpool.

'Leila...'

'No, shush, don't speak.'

'Leila, we should have done this years ago.'

Lee sat, holding Claudia from behind, on their top bunk. That was as intimate as it had got, with her frightful worry over the horses.

'You're not going out there,' he said, not for the first time. 'You'll catch your death.'

Another clash of thunder sounded above the fort.

'Those poor horses,' said Claudia.

'Claudia, they're as used to thunder as we are. What do proper horse-owners do during a storm? Nothing, probably.'

'This storm's ridiculous, though.'

'It'll be over soon.'

'I hate Texas.'

'I love Texas. I love Texas because you're in Texas.'

He eased her down to the mattress.

'Try to relax,' he said. 'You'll feel better in the morning.'

She was suddenly distressed for the two of them. 'But I want to make love to you.'

'Another time. We've got five great months yet, baby.'

By morning, the storm had thankfully moved away, and something was afoot with a group in the cookhouse. There was talk over breakfast, led surprisingly by Phil, about a fresh mission back to the graveyard in order to claim the missing letters from home. Kurt and Kevin were gung-ho for the idea – Andy and Jon less so.

'We're low on ammo,' Andy pointed out. 'If we use what we have at the graveyard, we could have big trouble if the main lot somehow get in to us.'

Kevin, with a history of dismissing other people's views, said, 'We'll just use the shovels. We were taken by surprise last time.'

'Yes, yes,' said Kurt, pounding the table.

'It's a long way,' pointed out Jon, 'through mud, after last night.'

'Ah, no,' said Phil. He was still in his Mets caps – perhaps thinking of baseball cheered him up. 'We go on the hand cart.'

'We go on the what?' asked Jon.

'The railway hand cart,' continued Phil. 'You know, where you have to pump the handle up and down.'

'Oh,' said Andy. 'That thing out there? From the old silent cowboy films.'

Gloria stumbled in, blurry eyed. She and Kurt smiled at each other. Lee followed in soon after. Glancing at the table of conspirators, he went up to Michelle and whispered in her ear. Michelle giggled, told him to wait a while. Lee wandered over to listen to the meeting.

'What was that?' Devin asked his wife.

'Man wanted to prepare breakfast in bed for Claudia. I said we'd be happy to put something together.'

Devin grinned. 'Nice thought. Honey, I'll do that for you one of these days.'

Michelle laughed, and slapped Devin on his big behind.

Once Lee realised what was being discussed, he thought of Claudia's letter, and volunteered.

'No more room on the hand cart,' said Kurt.

That was debatable.

Jon spotted a possible confrontation and said, 'Thinking about Claudia's letter? I'll look for it, Lee.'

'Thanks, Jon. Good luck out there, yeah. Be careful.'

Lee left them to it.

'Are we on, then?' asked Kevin. 'One more storm like that and there'll be nothing left to find. How about we leave in an hour?'

Jon was concerned with Phil's age. 'Phil should be the look-out. The rest of us should work the pump.'

Everyone agreed. Kurt finished his coffee before striding out to assess the hand cart. The other four remained eating.

'After this,' said Andy, 'we'll check our weapons. As Kevin says, use shovels if we find anything. Guns only as a last resort.'

Everyone nodded.

'Andy,' said Jon. 'I vote you're in charge of this today.'

'I second that,' said Phil.

It was a cold morning. Everyone gathered on the

cookhouse boardwalk once word spread of the mission. The hand cart had been worked onto the main track. Phil was making mental notes of who missed out the first time they visited the graveyard.

Prodilyn waved his query away. 'I'm not really bothered,' she said. 'Spend the time looking for other people's.'

That stance surprised some people.

Leila said to Phil, 'If you can get it, that would be great.'

'The same from me,' said Charlie.

Phil pointed at Lee and Claudia, remembering that Jon had that one covered, then he was hauled up onto the hand cart, where the handle was at the chests of Andy and Kurt, and the knees of Jon and Kevin.

'Good luck!' shouted Claudia, then, under her breath to Lee, 'Don't come back without my letter.'

Devin got the west gate open without being asked. The handle was see-sawed up and down and the cart moved slowly off.

'Put your backs into it!' shouted Claudia.

'Behave,' Lee told her, laughing with her. 'You're a disgrace, you are. Get back to bed.'

'Yes, sir.'

They finally made it out of the gate with a wave from Devin; then they were heading towards the bridge. Jon saw that the river was almost at flood levels – he was no expert, but he couldn't imagine a boat being risked until it subsided somewhat.

They kept up a steady pace, pumping up and down.

'Fuck me,' exclaimed Kevin. 'This is hard work. We don't go uphill, do we?'

'Save your breath, Kevin,' advised Andy.

'Zombie!' shouted Phil suddenly. 'Lone one, alongside the track.'

The pumping went all to cock with the excitement of the news.

'Keep rhythm,' called Andy. 'Phil, can you handle it?'

Phil picked up a shovel, turning it in his hands like a baseball player.

'Short jab,' advised Kevin. 'Don't swing through into one of us.'

They approached the zombie, a female wearing a ragged brown dress and with long black hair around the pale face. Jon and Kevin got the best view, facing forward as they were. Phil edged to the right side of the cart, with the shovel up in the air. At the critical moment he jabbed the cutting edge at her throat.

'Shot!' shouted Kevin.

The zombie gave out a loud, prolonged hiss but, overall, took the blow quite well and lunged at the passing cart.

'Shit!' from Kevin.

'Again, Phil!' shouted Andy.

Kurt was trying to work the handle and lean inwards at the same time. Phil brought up the shovel and clanked the zombie full in the face. She fell away, leaving them to pass freely.

'Sorry,' said Phil. 'I'll do better next time.'

'You'd better,' laughed Kevin. 'Or you'll be pumping this bleedin' thing.'

They reached the cemetery, the four on the handle puffing and blowing. Jon stood there daydreaming, actually feeling a little sad for the lone female zombie. He was brought out of his reverie by a military-style call to action from Andy, and he found himself ankle deep in mud, moving with his shovel towards the storm-battered cemetery.

'Stay there and keep your eyes open,' Andy said to Phil. 'I'll try your grave first.'

Kevin laughed as he walked. 'My word, "I'll try your grave first", classic.'

Kurt found his grave and went at it as if he were digging a fresh grave for Leland. Jon had to go further into the churned-up burial ground. He saw his headstone at a jaunty angle, and ignored both it and its contents. Instead, he searched for Leila and Claudia's resting places. He came across them alongside each other! Good. He lunged in with his shovel, doing both graves at the same time. Stinking, putrefied zombie corpses came up over his feet. He heard someone curse at their own hideous chore, then he saw part of an envelope, more on Leila's side. It looked completely sodden. He retrieved it, pocketed it and ploughed on.

A few minutes later, several things happened in a rush: Kurt had success, as did Jon with the other envelope, and a warning shout came from Phil. Everyone frantically looked to identify the threat, which proved to be a trio of zombies several hundred yards further along the track. Kevin had been looking for Charlie's letter in a rotten grave washed partly through the fence – he wasn't too upset to admit failure and take up a defensive position ahead of the cart.

Kurt and Jon were done. Filthy but pleased. They left the graveyard. The three zombies had been joined by three others from a gulley at the side of the track.

'Hey!' shouted Kevin.

Andy continued to look for Phil's envelope – a stout effort as other graves had merged into Phil's. Phil watched on with deepening concern.

'We should go, Andy!' called Jon.

Andy assessed the lumbering approach of the zombies and kept digging. Kevin shouldered his shovel and went looking for trouble. He closed the gap to the six zombies and pinged one flat out. What fun! The next one received the blade of the shovel up under the chin, virtually decapitating it. Another got chopped at a knee first, before Kevin wound himself up for a haymaker to the head.

'Kevin!' they all shouted as one from the cart. 'Look out!'

Kevin lost his cheesy grin at seeing extra zombies bearing down on him from the gulley. It was time to clear out, so he got his feet moving through the gloopy mud back towards the others.

'Andy!' called Jon. 'We have to go!'

Andy was forced to give up on Phil's letter, clearly upsetting the older man.

'I'm sorry, Phil,' said Andy, climbing aboard.

'I appreciate your efforts,' replied Phil.

Phil remained grim-faced on the cart as the others slowly got it moving back towards the fort.

GB Hope

TWENTY-TWO

Doc laughed out loud from the book he was reading, then had to deal with a mild coughing fit. The cookhouse was full and comfortable all round, with the fire ablaze, Charlie on the piano, Lee massaging Claudia's feet.

'Will you do my feet next?' Jon kidded him. 'Doc, what's so funny?'

'The worst zombie book ever written,' answered Doc. 'They're trapped at the start, as often happens in these books, apparently. They've begun discussing the best forms of suicide. One is saying to slit wrists, another wants to jump out of the window. What do you reckon? What's the best way to go?'

'I don't know,' said Jon.

Charlie had stopped playing the piano. Gloria turned and said to him, 'Charlie, you're a deep thinker. What's the best form of suicide?'

Charlie found he had an audience, like boy scouts around a camp fire. 'Depends how brave or unhinged you are. A gunshot to the head takes courage, but should be guaranteed. Slitting wrists without being drugged first would be painful. Jumping out of the window, one assumes, would be awful. My best bet would be pills. Maybe even better, if there's no great rush, to take away a lot of the fear and anxiety, would be to put one cyanide pill in with thirty other dummy pills. Take one a day for a month. That way, you may go after the third one, or the thirteenth.'

'If I was still alive after a month of doing that,' said Kevin, 'I'd blow my brains out!'

Everyone laughed heartily. 'Don't try to commit suicide that way in February,' continued Kevin. More laughter, then they settled back down into their quiet evening.

The three recovered letters had earlier sparked completely different results: Kurt's was from his mother in Gothenburg, Sweden. It was the usual guff, covering family love and support for his adventure and what the vet had done to the German Shepherd. What made it extraordinary was that the usually taciturn Kurt chose to read it out to the group. They gave him nice comments and a spattering of applause. As he sat down, no longer the centre of attention, Kurt wished his letter had been from his girlfriend back in Connecticut. He loved his mother, of course, but guilt had crept up on him, with the way he had sneaked away from Brook, left her without so much as a going away note. He wondered if she was all right; whether she had gone home to Iowa; if he would ever see her again.

Leila kept her letter within her immediate circle. It was from her friend Jo in Blackpool, the one who had brought Seamus back to their room when Jon was there. When Jon realised who it was from, he said, 'I waded through the detritus of a zombie corpse for a letter from that slapper?'

Claudia's envelope had been so ruined as to be illegible.

Because she had not been at all upset, Jon had joked, 'I waded through the detritus of a zombie corpse for nothing!'

Lee came in from the latrines, chilled to the bone – cold, cold Texas. The bunkhouse had some warmth from the stove in the hall, but Claudia had taken to sleeping in her clothes. He himself manned-up, continuing to sleep naked (or at least in his shorts), relying on her body heat to keep him alive. She was there on the top bunk, wearing a sweatshirt with *Yankees* written on it, and long black shorts. Her earphones were in and she giggled. She looked up at him. 'It always amuses me when Alicia Keys rhymes Brooklyn bridge with empty fridge.'

He shut the door and gestured for her to remove the phones.

She complied. 'Yes, baby?'

'I'm not tired in the slightest. Could we, if you wouldn't mind, you know...' He winked a couple of times and jiggled his right shoulder. 'Share an earpiece, listen to some Phil Collins?'

She laughed. 'I've got a treat for you. "Rodrigo guitar concerto". Ten minutes long.'

'Oh, deep joy.'

He quickly threw off his clothes under her smiling observation, climbed up and got under the blankets. There, he held her. She gave him a little kiss on the lips.

'Lee, after all this, can we go to England?'

'Well, we'll have that land as a prize, remember.'

'Oh, we'll go and see that. I mean, we'll own that, we can still go home for a while.'

'If you really want to.'

'It's a genealogy thing, darling. I want to set eyes on York, and other places that matter to me. It's a deep-set feeling for me. And then we can visit locations important to you.'

'That won't take long. We must go and see Huddersfield, though.'

'Why, what's Huddersfield to you?'

'Nothing. I've just always wanted to go to Huddersfield.'

He was winding her up. 'Now, stop it.'

She turned slightly towards him and wrapped a delicious leg around him through the blankets. Their faces were then closer, just to lose themselves in each other's eyes. They kissed again – deep and unhurried.

'Can I bathe this morning?' Claudia asked Lee.

Delicate moment, he thought. They were walking to the cookhouse, arm in arm, wrapped up against a freezing wind. He said, 'A bath?'

'I could always wait 'til spring.'

'I'll organise it after breakfast.'

They found everyone already there, looking like extras from the disaster movie, *The Day After Tomorrow*. Only Phil was absent. He had taken his breakfast and withdrawn to the solitude of the jail. Lee bid good morning to the faces looking their way. Devin and Michelle were, of course, their usual friendly selves.

'Devin, my friend,' said Lee, putting a hand on one of Devin's broad shoulders. 'You must forego your land prize and come and work for us.'

'Oh, no,' laughed Devin. 'We're going to open our own church mission. You can come and work for us.'

'What if they give you half of Alaska?'

'Then Alaska it will be.'

Claudia pulled Lee down to the seat next to her, wanting less chatter and more breakfast. He grinned at her sulky expression. Claudia looked at Leila chatting, up close and personal, with Jon. She saw Doc glance her way and smile. He looked a little better, with more colour in his face. He had actually cultivated his goatee beard. Leland was looking at her over his waffles. And Kurt was watching her without any food in front of him. He realised he was staring and looked away. The other way, Prodilyn and Gloria were engaged in washing pots in the sink. They were having an animated conversation and laughing a great deal.

Doc left the cookhouse, putting on his hat and closing his long leather coat. Like most of the men he was still in cowboy dress – he would feel lost without his gun tucked under his ribcage. Despite the biting wind he decided to move about the compound. He climbed a ladder to the west wall, so that he could observe the river, which was still high. It felt good to be up there, but the wind cut into his face, so he didn't linger long. He got down and moved slowly across the mud. At the jail he paused to speak with Phil, who was sitting smoking just inside the doorway.

'You all right, Phil?'

'Good, thank you, Doc.'

'You seem a little down with the place.'

'I'll come around.'

Doc indicated the noose. 'That thing still in place, I see.'

'Be silly to move it now, don't you think.'

'I suppose it would.'

Doc tipped his hat and moved on. It was good to see the Stars and Stripes and the State flag of Texas flying proudly over the main gate. At the stables he looked in on the horses. They eyeballed him back. They seemed well enough, and hopefully would be shipped out soon. In the shelter from the wind, Doc took out his wife's letter and re-read it for the hundredth time. He grinned as he imagined the time when he would be able to tell her how it was delivered.

He put the letter away as he headed to the bunkhouse. He planned to read a few chapters of his zombie book, which he was surprisingly quite into by then. On the way he passed Prodilyn and Gloria, lighting their stove in their commandeered building. One of them whistled at him, and then they moved to the open doorway to watch him go by.

'Ladies,' he said, in his best Southern drawl.

Doc smiled, thinking of them as Wild West prostitutes touting for business. He wondered, if he hadn't developed his chest infection, whether he would have been targeted like some of the other guys. And what would happen if he got himself back to full health? He fingered the letter in his pocket as he entered the bunkhouse.

Claudia had to wait for her bath, as Leland had the same plan. He did offer to defer to her but she wouldn't hear of it. Lee decided not to joke about the two of them sharing the tub, instead going back to the bunkhouse with Claudia for an hour. She spent the time putting her hair into pigtails, while he lay on the bottom bunk amongst discarded clothes, toiletries and a couple of zombie books.

'I'd kill for a bag of popcorn,' he said.

'You and your popcorn.'

'Do you think Devin and Michelle could make some? Assuming they've got corn.'

'Don't you think they do enough?'

'Did you hear what Charlie was talking about as we came away? He's going to put a quiz together for tonight.'

Claudia looked at him with her mouth agog. 'Have we reached that stage? Please, let me not be on your team.'

'What do you mean? I'll be good on sport. I'm an expert on the history of Manchester City FC. Oh, I didn't tell you, did I? When we get our land, I'm buying two big dogs and calling them Yaya and Toure.'

That was enough to make her get up and flop down onto him.

'Lee, what on earth are you talking about?'

They were there, so thought they might as well kiss for a moment.

'In honour of my all-time favourite City player, Yaya Toure. Big black guy, from the Ivory Coast. When he got going, no one could stop him.'

'I'm sure he'd be delighted to have your dogs named after him.' After a struggle, she freed herself from his embrace. 'Are you going to see if Leland's finished?'

Lee gave that some thought. 'Am I going to see if another bloke has got out of the bath yet?'

'Well, we're going, anyway, because I need the loo.'

As he tried to talk himself into getting to his feet, his eyes settled on Claudia's graveyard letter, which had dried into a mud-stained piece of origami. In particular he was looking at a part of the illegible text where the signature had stained through from the last page (before being later obliterated). It definitely said "your loving mother".

The letter was in his pocket before he stood up, taking Claudia's hand. As they got into their boots in the hallway, two things rushed round in his head: Claudia's mother was deceased, so the letter must be bogus or malicious in some way. And he wondered why he loved the juxtaposition of cold (from the doorway) and warmth (from the stove) so much. He wanted only to stay there and hold Claudia, but she was dragging him outside.

'Pee,' she said.

The bathhouse was warm and empty of any naked men. While Claudia went off to relieve herself, Lee set to boiling water. He filled a quarter of the tub with cold water.

'Are we ready?' asked Claudia, returning, and already stripping.

'A little patience, please. You're getting like Cleopatra.'

'If I smell like you, would you want to sleep with me?'

'Good point.'

They had to wait, so they hugged.

'We're the best couple here, aren't we?' she said.

He gave it some thought. 'Of course.'

'You can be on my quiz team tonight.'

He murmured his thanks. The water was bubbling. He took two hand towels and lifted the large pan, to pour hot water into the cold. Claudia checked the outcome with her elbow.

'Perfect,' she said.

He missed her getting naked as he put more water on the

boil. He brought over a chair and sat down. Someone was walking along the boardwalk to the door.

'Don't be alarmed!' called Lee. 'Naked people in here.'

Doc came in with his eyes averted, heading to the latrines. 'Don't mind me. You gotta go, you gotta go.'

Lee looked at Claudia as she bent over to wash her hair between her knees. Before Texas he had not realised how absolutely sexy her back was. It was a toned and marvellous sight.

Charlie wanted to have some fun, so he would ask questions to people individually, rather than have groups with pencils and paper. It was like an Old West *Weakest Link*. So, every man for himself, thought Lee. Probably better than him and Claudia being teamed up with Jon and Leila.

It was pitch black outside, blowing a gale, so everyone seemed keen to play, even the morose Phil. People settled down with their hot drinks and snacks, Devin and Michelle on the chaise longue, Gloria near to Kurt, Doc by the window – not a fan of quizzes but amused by the atmosphere. Charlie was sat at the piano, which was not a great position but everyone could see him.

'Shall we begin?' asked Charlie. 'We could go round alphabetically, but I can't be arsed thinking about that, so we'll start to my left and finish to my right. So, you're first, Mr Leland.'

Everyone laughed. Leland blushed a little.

'Here we go! Prisoner, Robert Stroud, was known as the what of Alcatraz?'

'The Birdman!' answered Leland, without hesitation.

Everyone cheered. Doc shook his head in amusement. He would be fourth after Kurt and Gloria. Charlie made a note of Leland's answer.

'Kurt,' said Charlie. Gloria rubbed Kurt's knee by way of encouragement. 'What was the nationality of the painter, Vincent Van Gogh?'

Kurt looked at Gloria, who desperately wanted to tell him. Then he gave it some thought and answered correctly. Gloria's applause was fairly cringe-worthy,

The first round of questions were fairly easy, and then they were back at Leland again.

'Leland, 'In the *Back To The Future* films, what was the name of Marty McFly's eccentric scientist companion?'

'Doc Brown,' answered Leland, like a fan.

Because there was nothing else to do, Charlie kept the game going for quite a long time. Jon and Lee seemed to be the two with the best general knowledge, much to the pretend chagrin of their respective girls, Leila and Claudia, and in the end they were named by Charlie after the final totting up as being in the top three.

'In third place,' called Charlie. 'It's Devin!' Applause and laughter all round. 'Runner up, we have... Lee!' More hilarity and a squeal of joy from Leila. 'And our winner is Jon!'

Charlie closed the evening's entertainment by reciting some real answers from the ITV programme *Family Fortunes*, a Sunday night British staple in the eighties and nineties, where two families tried to find answers to questions already voted on by the general public. 'Name something you wouldn't expect to see in a strip joint: "Animals". A nickname for a slim person: "Slimmy". Something a Frenchman would say: "En Garde". Giggles turned to guffaws at that one. 'A food that can be easily eaten without chewing: "Chips". A bird with a long neck: "Naomi Campbell". A way of toasting someone: "Over a fire". Two famous brothers: "Bonnie and Clyde". Something you shouldn't even try once: "Sex on a train". A game you can play in the bath: "Scuba diving".'

TWENTY-THREE

Leila and Jon lay entwined in her bunk, reading *Forty Things I Want To Tell You* by Alice Kuipers, on the Kindle borrowed from Claudia. Leila was naked, but he had on a Kings of Leon tee-shirt and a black beanie hat with the white logo for Tottenham Hotspurs FC on the front – feeling the cold that night. She looked quizzically at the hat and he pulled an "Am I bovvered?" expression. His attire didn't particularly matter – in the real world they would already be making love, but in the fort, where time meant nothing, they would move into intimacy later in the night.

'Are you enjoying the book?' she asked.

'Sort of. My nine-year-old niece reads quicker than you.'

'Sorry.'

'Your Charlie was funny tonight.'

'Yes, you wouldn't expect it from him, would you?'

'He's doing a piano recital tomorrow night.'

'Shut up.'

He did shut up and focussed on looking at her profile. The flashing of her long eyelashes suggested she was conscious of his gaze.

'Jon, you know this land we're getting? Do you think we'll

be near to each other.'

'I hadn't thought about it. Probably not.'

'Could we ask them to sort it out?'

'I can't really imagine that conversation.'

'But, what if I'm in New York and you're in, say, Pennsylvania, or somewhere?'

'Let's see what happens.'

'Do you not see a future for us?'

'Of course I do. But...'

'Oh, you're thinking about me and Lee in the shopping mall. I was a girl then. Now I'm a woman.'

'A very beautiful woman.'

'I want you, Jon. I won't change my mind.'

'And I want you. If it comes down to it, you sell your land and move in with me.'

She went quiet for a while. He wondered if he had upset her.

'I don't like the sound of Pennsylvania,' she said.

He laughed. 'Then New York State it is.'

'Good.'

Prodilyn didn't really go in for climbing ladders much, but she went up one to join Charlie on the west wall. He saw her coming. He was surprised – she'd hardly said two words to him since boarding the train.

'Looking for the boat?' she asked.

'Not particularly. I've got twenty-four hours a day in here, so I like to use an hour up here. It's very fresh, and a nice view. Sometimes, I fantasise that I'm a cavalryman on sentry duty, looking for Indians.'

Prodilyn smiled. 'I thought it was because you didn't like looking at the zombies on the other side.'

'Perhaps that's part of it as well.'

'You were very good with the quiz the other night. You'll have to do it again.'

'I may just do that. How's things going in here with you, Prodilyn?'

'Still a bit strange. I might go through the whole thing and not feel comfortable with it at all. Maybe I need my own place for an hour each day.'

'It's a long wall.'

They stood in silence for a couple of minutes.

'I believe you shared a house with Leila in Blackpool?' Prodilyn asked. 'Did she ever speak of the other event?'

Charlie looked at Prodilyn, appearing pleasant and relaxed in his company, yet he remembered his earlier impressions of her, as someone he wouldn't normally trust. He put it down to his years in the police.

'No,' he lied. 'She was very tight lipped about it all.'

Another minute passed.

'Have you been to America before?' asked Charlie.

'Oh, yeah, we had a h— holiday here a few times.' She tried to corral her hair in the wind. 'Charlie, I wanted to ask you. You said something to Gloria a while back. About life after death. It's just that I lost someone recently. Well, who didn't? I just wanted to hear the idea for myself.'

So, Charlie repeated what he had said, about the meaningless futility of a new-born baby dying, but then continuing to live on in a different strand, where everything was normal and beautiful, where life was as it should have been, knowing and being known by siblings, and outliving parents. Prodilyn listened, thinking about the loss of her husband, and imagining going on with him in a parallel universe – making love, arguing, moving house, making business decisions. She digested it all as she looked off into the distance. But then the wind had frozen her face, so she thanked Charlie, even touched his arm, and descended the ladder to get inside.

Lee found himself alongside Jon at the urinals in the latrines.

'Jon, I've been looking for you.'

'Have you, indeed?'

'There's something I want to show you.' Jon looked slowly sideways at Lee. 'Oh, no, no, not that. Can I come to your room?'

They both laughed. Jon gestured for Lee to follow him out.

Jon led Lee into his room in the bunkhouse, then closed the door and sat down on the lower bunk.

'What's on your mind?' asked Jon.

'Do you find it a problem getting to your zip because of the gun belt?'

'All my life. But I have button-fly.'

Lee then became serious as he brought Claudia's letter from his pocket and handed it over.

'It dried out,' said Lee. 'If you look there, the signature part has left an imprint on another page. Can you see?'

'Right, Claudia's mother. That's a shame. But...?

'Well, it is a shame, because Claudia's mother is dead.'

Jon made a surprised face. 'Are you sure?'

'I'm positive. I've seen her grave in York. I've spoken to relatives in Connecticut. I would believe Claudia's word without any of that, anyway.'

'No doubt you would. How bizarre, mate. Sit down.'

Lee sat alongside Jon, watching the man puzzle over the letter.

'So, it's malicious?' said Jon.

'Looks like it.'

'But why? Everyone else seemed happy with their letter. You were, weren't you?'

Lee thought of his father. 'Well, yeah. It was genuine, at least.'

'Maybe it's from a relative, who at the top of the letter said "this is what your mother would have said to you if she was still with us".'

'That's one idea, Jon, but it's a bit far-fetched.'

'True. Maybe it's nothing personal. Perhaps the organisers of this thing wanted to stir up some trouble in here, and picked on Claudia at random. Has she seen this?'

'No.'

'I wouldn't show it to her, then, and you should let it go. It will just drive you nuts and you can't solve it.'

'You're right. Just strange, though.'

Prodilyn settled down with Gloria for another long day in their office cabin. From her position in a leather chair she could see the overcast sky to the north, the north wall, and anyone who walked alongside the bunkhouse in the direction of the stables or the main gate. She was trying to think through what Charlie had said to her, as the insatiable Gloria continued to witter on about the men in the fort. Gloria had exhausted the topics of beauty procedures and West End wine bars, but never got tired of discussing their male companions.

'Why did they let couples come in here?' asked Gloria. 'Lee's quite hot. It's a shame he's spoken for.'

Prodilyn shot her a look.

'Oh, sorry,' said Gloria. Lee was out of bounds in that way. 'I forgot. My mind's starting to wander. What's in that safe?'

Prodilyn looked over her shoulder at a black metal, period safe, about the size of a small refrigerator, sitting in a corner. She had not noticed it before.

Gloria, still on her feet, approached it, squatted down and twiddled the combination dial. 'I wonder what the combination is.'

Prodilyn got to her feet. 'I wonder why it's here at all. Shout your Kurt.'

Gloria did as she was told. Kurt, talking on the cookhouse boardwalk with Kevin, wandered over. For want of something better to do, Kevin went too, taking his coffee cup with him.

The two men's boots reverberated on the wooden floor as they entered the room.

'Is there a problem, ladies?' asked Kevin.

Prodilyn told them she was interested in the contents of the safe, and they both twiddled the dial.

'We can all do that!' said Prodilyn, with a little petulant tut. 'Can you blow it open?'

'With what?' asked Kurt.

'Can't you open some bullets and sprinkle gunpowder on the lock, or something?'

'Fucking hell,' said Kevin, aghast. 'We might blow our

hands off, that's about all.'

Prodilyn's expression suggested, back in the old, real world, she would have gone off on one by then. She looked at the two useless men, but persevered in getting what she wanted, somehow.

'Could you get together with the other boys and discuss it?'

Lee happened to be passing by, heading to the stables to look for Claudia. Kurt hailed him, more as a way to escape Prodilyn's stupidity, than expecting any real help.

Lee stepped up into the office, his first time ever in there.

'Lee,' said Kevin, 'We want to open that safe over there. Any ideas, mate?'

Lee stepped over to it, took a knee, and tried the handle at the side of the dial. The safe swung open. The girls screamed with delight, Kevin laughed uproariously and Kurt went on his way. There were only four things inside the safe: two shot glasses and two bottles of Jim Beam bourbon.

'Bottoms up,' said Lee.

Gloria squealed again and took the bottle as she kissed Lee on the cheek.

'Party!' cried Gloria. She fondled the bottle for a moment, before handing it to Kevin. 'Crack the seal, please, Kevin.'

'Glad to,' said Kevin, putting down his cup.

Lee made to leave.

'Won't you join us for a tipple?' asked Prodilyn.

'No, thank you,' said Lee. 'I'll be on my way.'

'Back to the little woman?' asked Gloria.

'Something like that.'

Lee made himself scarce. Kevin threw what was left of his

coffee out of the window and poured a shot of bourbon into his cup, then filled the shot glasses, which Prodilyn and Gloria picked up. They all savoured their first alcohol for over a month. Prodilyn gasped, while Kevin made a long noise of satisfaction.

'Shall we invite anyone else in?' asked Gloria. She shook her head with the other two. 'More for us, yeah!'

They hammered the whiskey straight off. Kevin was a big man and he could take it, but the two women were quickly on the way to being drunk, the situation possibly made worse by their abstinence in recent weeks. Laughing and joking, the three of them spilled out onto the boardwalk as if it were an Essex pub on a Friday night, shouting salutes to Doc at the bunkhouse door, and to Leland coming back from the latrines.

Phil watched the performance from the jailhouse door, and Charlie came out of the cookhouse to see what the commotion was.

'Don't worry, Charlie!' called Gloria. 'I'm on a different plane, I'm not here, drunk as a skunk.'

Prodilyn laughed hilariously. Kevin filled their glasses again – his wife back in the West Midlands was quite plain, so he was enjoying playing with these two hotties.

It was then that Claudia and Lee came out of the stables. They were laughing over the names she had given to the horses.

'I like the one you've called Amelie,' he said. 'What were the others? Aubrey? That's a strange name.'

'That one reminds me of a girl I went to college with. Really stupid.'

'Naomi and Ashley?'

'Ugly aunts back in Yorkshire. Big teeth – Naomi, and big bum – Ashley.'

Gloria spotted them and very loudly heckled Claudia, although it was mostly unintelligible gibberish.

'What did you say?' Claudia asked her in an aggressive tone.

'Claudia, darling!' shouted Gloria.

'Are they pissed?' Claudia asked Lee.

'Well spotted,' he replied.

'Claudia, darling!' shouted Gloria again. 'Why won't you let Lee come out to play?'

Uh-oh, thought Lee, reaching for Claudia's arm, but missing as she veered off towards Gloria.

'You're stif... stifling him, girl. You're making him a very dull boy.'

'Claudia, leave it,' said Lee.

'They shouldn't have put couples in here,' pontificated Gloria once again, pointing her empty glass at Claudia. 'It's not on, I tell you.'

'Come down here, slapper!' demanded Claudia.

Nobody stopped Gloria descending the three steps to face up Claudia.

'What's on your fucking mind?' Claudia asked her.

Gloria pointed at Lee. 'You don't deserve him.'

'You've got all these single men in here. What are you, a nymphomaniac, or something? You're a daft bitch, I know that!'

'Who are you calling a daft bitch?'

'Clearly, I'm calling you a daft bitch!'

Enough with the preliminaries – Gloria went for Claudia's eyes with her nails, and Claudia went for Gloria's hair. Gloria missed. Claudia got a good hold with her left hand, yanking Gloria around and punching her in the face several times with her right hand. Grappling ensued, Gloria put in a few slaps to Claudia's face, as she squealed and got pulled about by the hair. Lee tried to step in, but Claudia was in a frenzy of hair pulling and kicking. Kevin just stood there grinning, highly entertained, so Lee had to wait for Doc to come across to take hold of Gloria. In the time between, the two girls scratched, slapped, punched and kicked, and finally collapsed into the mud. Lee was down on his knees trying to pull his girlfriend clear.

At last they were separated. A bleeding and bedraggled Gloria was taken into the office and plonked down in a leather chair. Claudia had to be half-carried, screaming and kicking, to the bunkhouse. Lee got her into their room, where she at once regained her composure. She attempted to put her hair in some sort of order, and assessed her mud-splattered jeans. Then she looked at a panting, amused Lee.

'And in the red corner,' said Lee, 'Fighting out of New Milford, USA...'

TWENTY-FOUR

Claudia's last fight had been with a girl called Katie Sidebottom, at high school in York. Afterwards, it was awkward seeing the girl around school, but as they didn't have any corresponding lessons or interests, it was tolerable. Inside the old Texas fort, with its limited living space, the situation was a completely different kettle of fish. Gloria sported a glorious black eye, and a wounded persona. There was not a prayer for even the slightest conciliation or communication between the two of them, and anyone who dared to speak to one girl received a black look from the other. In general, the atmosphere was as leaden as the overcast weather.

Claudia and Lee sat in the cookhouse, having scrambled eggs, giant pancakes and coffee for breakfast.

'I'm sorry,' she said, turning her doleful eyes up to him.

'I should think so,' he kidded.

Everyone was with them in the room, with rain spitting against the windows. There had been no open discussions about what had happened, but clearly a division of sorts had opened up. It was like school, thought Claudia. Mumbled conversation and bad vibes came out of Gloria.

'I've caused problems,' Claudia said to Lee. 'After the way

things went wrong in the shopping mall, that's the last thing we need.'

Lee sipped his coffee. He now took it black like a real cowboy. 'The mall was completely different. Much heavier than this. Give it a couple of days and nobody will even remember the fight. I might, though, and tell our grandchildren about it.'

She smiled.

'All right,' he continued, 'Gloria won't ever talk to you again, but we can live with that.'

'I wanted it to be a better experience for us. A stress free one.'

'It still will be. You can't account for stupid people like her being put in here with us.'

'I love you, Lee.'

'I love you, too.'

Not everyone subscribed to the bad mood of the place – Jon and Leila were simply loved-up. It had turned into a kind of surreal *Carry on Camping* for them. Days merged into nights; talking, happily completing cookhouse chores, joking around, necking at every opportunity, planning for life afterwards, making love.

They did it every which way but loose. She became the most important thing ever in his life. She laughed when he told that fact to her. They were prostrate on her bunk at the time, one morning. With the tip of his right index finger he played with her smirking lips, touched her perfectly white front teeth, then went up over her philtrum. She wiggled her nose.

'I've got an itch needs scratching,' she said.

He ignored her, tracing instead over the bridge of her freckly nose.

'What *are* you doing?' she asked.

'I love your face. Your face fascinates me.'

'You're easily entertained.'

They found they were giggling over absolutely nothing.

'Leila, don't you think our bodies are compatible?'

Her laughter made her bare breasts bounce against his bare chest above her.

'Our bodies are *what?*'

'How can I explain?'

'I'm not sure I want you to.'

'I've been with women, yeah, good-looking and all that, and the sex was great.' She pulled a disgusted face. 'But there was always something a bit awkward. A bit wrong.'

'Maybe you're gay.'

'But with you I feel totally at ease.'

'Jon, are you saying, I complete you?'

Laughing again, they almost failed to hear the shouting coming from the compound. They paused, cocking ears.

'What was that?' asked Leila.

A shout came again. Jon jumped out of bed.

'Fire!' he said.

'Shit!'

She followed him to the floor and they grappled with clothing. In the corridor they bumped into Leland and Doc, then outside the first thing they saw was Devin and Michelle hustling by with buckets of water sploshing at their feet.

'Jon, it's the stables!' cried Leila, taking to her heels.

Jon went after her, seeing the blaze engulfing the rear of the stable block and part of the east wall. Claudia overtook him at a sprint, and then Lee was at his side, still in the action of dressing. Lee was calling for Claudia to wait, but she only had thoughts for the horses.

Andy and Kevin appeared with a bin full of water, carried between them. Kurt, it seemed, was the primary fire fighter, taking charge of the water as it arrived and throwing it onto the fire. The rising black smoke was disconcerting, but it was obviously not an inferno, especially after all the recent rain.

An odd couple of Prodilyn and Charlie were already rescuing the horses. Leila, and then Claudia, joined up with them and pulled Ashley, Naomi, Amelie and Aubrey from the stables and right to the other side of the fort.

Jon and Lee had arrived at the stable doors, ready to play their part in putting out the fire, but their role changed in a terrifying instant, as burning zombies began to infiltrate through the damaged wall. Their simultaneous obscenities were lost in the crackle of the blaze. Jon reached for his pistol and only came up with a handful of trouser leg. Lee was wearing his gun belt, but as he knew he was out of ammo, he frantically searched the stables for weapons. A heavy broom came to hand, not the most inspiring weapon. He had to take it and wield it at the zombie heads which were disgustingly ablaze. Jon found a pitchfork, which proved more useful, sticking zombies through the face, heaving them aside, before withdrawing the spikes with a foot on the chest like a soldier bayoneting. Gunshots rang out from Andy. Zombies dropped into mini-pyres.

Everyone in the fort was involved by then, even Gloria,

either bringing water or attacking the invaders. When Kurt joined the ranks of the fighters it was clear that the fire was under control. He shot and kicked out at those zombies that continued to stumble through the smouldering breach.

Then suddenly there came calm. People stood around, panting, dealing with their adrenalin rush. Kevin waded through zombie bodies to examine the damaged wall.

'Clear for the moment!' he shouted.

'We have to close that up!' shouted Prodilyn, one level down from hysterical.

Jon looked at Lee. 'State the bleedin' obvious,' he said.

'The covered wagon,' said Andy.

All the men immediately went for the wagon and dragged it out of the stables. Kurt put all his strength into it – the fact that it was his home suggested he felt to blame for the fire breaking out. The wagon was pulled between the stable block and the hole in the wall. It was rocked back and forth, back and forth, until it went over with a great crash and churning up of ground. The men stood looking at it, pleased that it solved the problem instantly.

'Is it enough?' asked Kevin.

'We can add to it,' said Andy.

'Let's check everyone's okay,' suggested Devin.

That was agreed upon. A head count was taken, during which Kurt finally admitted his carelessness with a paraffin lamp had started the fire. A number of voices told him not to worry, although Prodilyn looked like she wanted to kill him. She held her tongue, as Gloria linked arms with her.

'Let's reinforce that barrier,' said Kurt, keen to leave the group.

Devin, Andy and Kevin went with him. Jon and Lee left the scene to check on their women, standing with the horses near the cookhouse. Lee kissed Claudia on her cheek, Jon copied him with Leila.

'They seem none the worse,' said Lee.

'Fucking beyond a joke,' said Claudia. 'If that boat's not here within forty-eight hours, then we're riding these horses out of here. We'll get them to Barbra's ranch.'

'Stay calm, babe,' said Lee. 'It'll be here. Meantime, we'll build them a shelter.'

'Too right,' put in Jon.

Lee was stroking the nearest horse's face. He didn't know one from the other, but quipped, 'Amelie's a rough girl. She doesn't mind a little drama. And Aubrey hasn't got a clue what's going on.'

Lee saw Jon staring at him as if he were mad. He just gave him a wink.

Kurt worked like a Trojan to build a wooden shelter for the horses. It was between the bunkhouse and the north wall. Kevin and Charlie were the two men with the practical skills in carpentry to work with him, and it was ready by mid afternoon. Claudia assessed the structure with the cold eye of a bumptious council official, before giving it her approval.

Devin and Michelle kept the food going all day – their response to such a traumatic event. People sat quietly in the cookhouse. Jon and Leila enjoyed the best fried chicken of their lives, then went back to bed.

Kurt was not asked to explain the fire to anyone. He sat for a time with his own thoughts, only looking up when

Leland stood in front of him.

'Your bunk's there for you, man,' said Leland.

'Thank you, Leland.'

The mini-reconciliation was witnessed by Gloria on one side, and Lee and Claudia on the other. Lee couldn't help but be amused by the two women showing it exactly the same amount of disdain.

GB Hope

TWENTY-FIVE

Claudia's two day deadline over the welfare of the horses proved to be an intense period in the fort. Leila was far too involved with Jon to help at the makeshift stables, so Claudia was grateful to Kurt for lending a hand – clearly he felt responsible for the situation.

Claudia watched him finish the mucking out, steam actually rising from his head on the cold, early morning. 'You're much more help than Leila,' she joked.

Kurt grinned. 'It's my pleasure.'

'You should smile more, it suits you.'

'Ah, maybe.'

'Definitely. You're a good-looking guy. No need to be so deep all the time.'

He ran a finger across his sweaty brow and flicked it to the side, then gave Claudia his best blue-eyed, male model stare. For just a moment, her hormones made her forget that she loved Lee, and she allowed herself to fantasise about the gorgeous Swedish boy. Then she caught herself, and readied to go and clean up.

'I'd better have a wash,' she said. 'Before breakfast.'

She left him standing there, intently watching her go.

To that point so far, Doc's professional services had been limited to tending Leila's feet after the zombie attack and dealing with a couple of burnt fingers on Kurt's left hand following the fire. Apart from that, he had been his own patient, with his chest infection.

Gloria came running for him, saying Prodilyn had suffered a little accident in their room. He rushed off with her, collecting his medical bag from his own room. He could hear Prodilyn whimpering even from the bunkhouse corridor. Going into the room he found her lying face down on the bottom bunk, crying into the pillow, her jet black hair wildly covering her face. She wore a green goalkeeper's jersey, apparently her nightwear when not entertaining company, out of which her long, sleek legs projected, kicking once or twice with the pain of whatever ailed her. Doc knelt by the side of the bunk beds.

'Prodilyn, what's wrong?' he asked. He glanced back at Gloria, framed in the doorway. 'Thank you, Gloria. I've got it from here.'

'Oh, right you are,' said Gloria, closing the door after her.

Prodilyn's left eye emerged through her hair.

'I was climbing off the bunk,' she said, while sniffling. 'I'm up there. Getting down, I caught myself. Really bad pain.'

'What do you mean? Have you pulled something?'

'No, no, the bed cracked. I've got a splinter in me.'

'I understand.'

'Help me, Doc. It really hurts.'

'Okay. We'll have to take a look. Is it your leg? Your thigh?'

'My bum.'

'Oh. Let's get it over with, shall we?'

Doc gently lifted the tee-shirt up Prodilyn's back, revealing a heavy bloodstain on the left side of her white panties, and out of the middle of the stain stood a thick splinter of wood, resembling a chopstick. Doc found it to be a mildly amusing sight. He also noticed Prodilyn's sexily-toned lower back, before shaking his head to clear unprofessional thoughts.

'Ooh,' he said. 'Quite nasty. I'm going to have to cut your knickers off.'

'If you must.'

Doc fetched out scissors from his bag and carried out minor surgery on Prodilyn's underwear, carefully cutting around the foreign body until all the fabric fell to the sides. Doc's immediate considered diagnosis was... that Prodilyn had a gorgeous little butt. Actually, he couldn't find the words in his head to describe the curvy, erotic wonderfulness of it. If it didn't have a splinter sticking out of it, it would need... *Stop it, Doc*. He shook his head again and focussed on the wound. He touched the splinter.

'It hurts so bad, Doc.'

'I'm sure it does.'

There was nothing to be done except remove the offending item. Doc just hoped it all came out in one intact piece.

'This is going to hurt a bit, Prodilyn.'

'Oh, God.'

'It's got to come out. I'll do it quick.'

He took a hold on the splinter, Prodilyn cried out in pain,

and then he withdrew it in one swift movement, accompanied by a scream, plus the crying into the pillow and the pummelling of the feet on the bed. Doc threw the splinter away and examined the wound. Prodilyn looked at him; he pulled an "I've seen worse" doctor's expression, before going to his bag for disinfectant and a wad of cotton wool.

'Will I have a scar?' asked Prodilyn.

As he cleaned the wound, Doc saw no point in telling her the truth. 'No, I shouldn't think so. I think you need a couple of stitches, though.'

Prodilyn tried to stop crying and made some attempt to get her hair off her face. She lifted up onto her elbows and looked back in a coquettish fashion at Doc, who was trying to thread a surgical needle.

'This is so embarrassing,' she said.

'Accidents will happen.'

'Such a stupid thing to do. Do you want me in a different position?'

'No, you're fine where you are.'

He was ready to stitch the wound.

'This will hurt again,' he told her.

'Okay, Doc. I'll have to accept that you're going to hurt me.'

Doc paused and looked at her for a moment, then went to work, quickly closing the wound while Prodilyn whimpered and squirmed. After that, he taped a gauze pad in place and stood up.

'I'll send Gloria in,' he said, placing a tablet bottle beside her and closing his bag. 'Antibiotics there. Two a day.'

'Yes, Doctor. Thank you.'

He had to look back at the image on the bed as he left the room.

Doc was surprised that Prodilyn's injury hadn't become the talk of the cookhouse, especially with that scream at one point, and with Gloria not exactly being the soul of discretion. But it remained confidential. Prodilyn came into the cookhouse that evening, smiled at him and sat down gingerly on her right side, keeping her wounded buttock off the seat.

Gloria ran around after Prodilyn, which wasn't anything new, so nobody took any special notice. Later in the evening, Doc checked on his patient. She invited him to sit with her.

'How are you feeling?'

'It's not too bad. But, there does seem to be something still in there.'

'Really? It came out very cleanly.'

'Perhaps you could take another look.'

'Of course. Now?'

'I'm sure there's no great panic. Before we turn in?'

'Very well.'

'I meant to ask, Doc, where did you practise medicine?'

'Chicago most recently. Before that, Sandusky, Ohio. That's where my wife comes from.'

'You've left your wife in Chicago?'

Doc crossed his legs and caressed his goatee, deep in thought. 'Yes. It seems for such a long time.'

'It'll fly by, trust me.'

Michelle was preparing cocoa for everyone who wanted some. Prodilyn waved and nodded when Michelle checked with her. Doc declined.

'It's like a retirement home,' said Prodilyn. 'Cocoa before bed.'

It was Andy who was passing out the steaming mugs of cocoa. He placed Prodilyn's down beside her on a table. 'There you go, Mrs Hester. Doc, are you sure you don't want any?'

Doc had drifted off into a reverie over his wife. 'Sorry, what?'

'Cocoa, Doc. Are you sure you don't want any?'

'Oh, no, thank you.'

Prodilyn suddenly made a move, standing with a grimace. 'I'm tired, Doc. Shall we do that examination?'

Doc stood. 'Surely. I'll carry your drink.'

'No, leave it, I've changed my mind.'

They walked to the bunkhouse. There came the sound of snoring, somebody had turned in very early. Doc picked up his medical bag from his room, before following Prodilyn into hers, and shut the door behind them. Doc's mind was in a whirl. He was fully aware that he was acting in an unprofessional way, guilty over his wife, but excited to be alone with Prodilyn in her room.

His anxiety moved to another level as she began to prepare herself for the examination, carefully bringing down her sweatpants over the bandage, then slipping them down her legs and stepping out of them. Doc realised she was naked from the waist down. At least she was turned to the side, but it was still an extremely erotic sight. She was looking at him sideways, a few strands of hair down across her left cheekbone, before she crawled onto the lower bunk on her hands and knees, and lowered herself down.

Doc approached and knelt beside her. She pulled her hair up and over to the side of her head, away from him. Doc was faced with Prodilyn's pert bottom. Annoyed at his own silliness, of his guilty feelings, he peeled away the tape holding the gauze. He examined the wound.

'How does it look?' asked Prodilyn.

As he touched her skin around the entry point she gave out a little gasp of pain. He thought she was putting it on.

'I'm happy with it,' he proclaimed. 'I'll change the dressing while I'm here. Then we'll monitor it for a while.'

'Very good, Doc.'

Doc redressed the injury. He would have told her then, if she were a normal patient, that she could cover up, but of course she had nothing to cover herself with.

'Thank you, Doc. You've been very kind.'

He gestured that it was all in a day's work.

'You don't have to rush off, do you?' she asked.

'I beg your pardon?'

'I wondered if we could chat for a while. It's just, I'm so used to late night television, or being out in a club, nights in this place mess with my head. The silence, you understand. It's as silent as the grave in here.'

'I can't imagine it being very quiet with Gloria.'

'There is that, I suppose. But she babbles on for a while, then suddenly she's out like a light. Like somebody hypnotises her.'

Doc remembered that he was talking with an attractive woman who was not his beloved wife, in her bedroom, with her naked bottom right there.

She read his mind, laughing a little. 'I'm not bothered, if

241

you're not. I know this is unusual, Doc, but we're all friends here, aren't we?'

'I'm not overly bothered, Prodilyn.'

She changed position slightly, bringing her left knee up, and in so doing putting an erotic crease between her thigh and her torso.

'I like having you in here, Doc. I would have invited you earlier, only you've been poorly.'

On cue, he gave a little nervous cough.

She suddenly laughed, 'I can't believe I speared myself in the ass.' She paused, taking her time over becoming serious. 'Will you let me show my appreciation for your excellent care?'

'Errm, I don't know about that, Prodilyn.'

Her hand reached out to his right thigh. 'Please, Doc.' His head was slowly shaking, but it might have been slowly nodding.'

'You're not really in any condition,' he said.

'Oh, I disagree. I'm sure you'll be gentle with me.'

Subconsciously, Doc had reached up to touch his goatee. Her bare bottom, it was right there.

TWENTY-SIX

The morning brought with it a heavy fog – quite a ghostly novelty for everybody in the fort, as they wrapped up warm and drifted towards breakfast in the cookhouse. Gloria, forced to stay up late due to her room mate's activities, slept in, so Prodilyn entered the cookhouse alone. She stood in the doorway and smiled at Doc, who sat there cuddling a cup of coffee. He acknowledged her, but chose not to alter the set of his face.

She didn't join him at his table, but still, individually, they relived the previous night. The sex (not lovemaking, just sex) had been a mixture of base animalism, embarrassment and hilarity – embarrassment on his part, and the hilarity because they were careful not to inflame her injury. She had needed to be on top at all times, and found her normally expert technique severely handicapped by a throbbing backside.

Leland and Jon were discussing the possibility of holding an archery tournament. They wondered what they could make targets out of. Zombies were immediately disregarded because they wouldn't stay still. Leland came up with the idea of painting rings on the side of a building. Jon questioned where they could lay hands on paint.

'Only you two,' said Leila, slouched over her bowl of porridge, 'could decide on an archery tournament on the foggiest day of the year.'

Jon looked at Leland. 'Harsh. She's very harsh.'

Phil and Charlie had begun yet another chess match. Andy sat alone, eating toast.

Doc stood up and slipped into his coat. He surreptitiously checked on his patient as he headed off to the latrines.

'Are you sore?' he asked.

'Extremely,' she said, naughtily.

'I meant your injury.'

'That too.'

He gave an astonished expression before leaving.

Lee also slept in late. At least once during their stay, he was sure, he had offered to help Claudia with the horses, but she could tell he wasn't keen, so never mentioned the subject in front of him.

Claudia had been the first to walk out into the fog, giving a whoop of joy because she liked that particular kind of weather phenomenon. She was joined for breakfast by a yawning Kurt. Amusingly, she found him even more monosyllabic than usual, so let him wake up in his own time.

They walked together to the makeshift stables. She said good morning to Ashley, Naomi, Aubrey and Amelie, while he leant on his pitchfork and rubbed his eyes.

They got on with their chores. Kurt moved about in a lethargic manner, clearly not in the mood for manual labour. He paused to watch Claudia, impressed as always with her. Her back was to him, her ponytail flailing from side to side. In his opinion she possessed a marvellous physique, and then she had cause to bend, revealing the skin of her lower back.

'What made you leave Sweden, Kurt?' she asked, over her shoulder. He failed to answer, so she turned with a smile. 'You never stop gabbing, do you, Kurt?'

'Gabbing?'

'Talking. So, go on, why were you in the US?'

'I had to get out of town quick.'

'Really? What were you running away from, a shotgun wedding?'

'A what?'

'Never mind.'

'I was wanted by the police.'

'The police? Whatever for?'

'Nothing, really.'

'You don't flee to another country unless it's something serious.'

She suddenly had an image of Michael Corleone fleeing to Sicily after gunning down the police captain and Sollozzo the Turk in *The Godfather*.

Kurt didn't have a problem telling her. 'I led a gang in southern Sweden and Denmark. We'd ride motorbikes into shopping arcades and raid jewellery shops. We did twenty-four jobs, in total.'

'Wow. Did you ever work in England? I saw that kind of thing on the news once.'

Aubrey decided for some reason to get frisky, moving sideways and bumping Claudia towards the wall. Kurt moved quickly to pull her clear. While in Kurt's arms, Claudia giggled and slapped the horse's flank.

'You bad girl,' she said, then to Kurt, 'Well, well, an armed robber.'

She laughed at his shocking revelation; this pretty boy with his model looks – cool, emotionless features. She failed to notice that beneath his calm exterior he was maddened for her, that having his hands on her waist and her legs against his, and her beautiful smile so near to his face, he wanted her completely. He kissed her on the mouth. She was so surprised that she allowed it to continue for a moment, before breaking the bond of their lips.

'Nice,' she joked. 'But not on, Kurt.'

She expected him to release her, to apologise for forgetting himself, then they could laugh it off. But he went in again for further kissing.

'Kurt!' She turned her face away. 'Pack it in, will you!'

He wouldn't stop. He couldn't stop. Claudia immediately became livid with his advances and his wandering hands. He was kissing her face and neck, then took a firm hold on her hair to be able to bring her face to the front where he could force her lips apart with his tongue.

Even though he was inflamed with lust, Kurt still had enough of his wits about him to expect her to raise her knee towards his groin, so when it came he took it on his muscular right thigh. It was enough, though, to unbalance him, and she could break the hold and stumble away.

'Fuck off!' she screamed at him. 'What do you think you're fucking doing!?' Amazingly his face remained impassive. He followed her out to the side of the bunkhouse.

'Will you fuck off!?'

Shock made Claudia stumble backwards onto her rear in

the mud. Kurt watched her go down, then his gaze lifted up and beyond. Lee was there. There was no confusion in Lee's face. The situation was plain. He advanced beyond his seated girlfriend towards Kurt. If they had been inside a building or on a dry surface he would have swept Kurt's legs from under him and choked the man unconscious, even to death if nobody stopped him. But in the cloying mud he couldn't close the gap very quickly. Claudia cried out for him not to do anything drastic – Kurt at least raised his hands as if to say the whole thing had been a misunderstanding.

Without thinking, Lee drew his Colt pistol and pointed it at Kurt's forehead, some six inches away.

'No!' screamed Claudia.

By then, the disturbance had brought out other people: Prodilyn and Doc, Kevin, Charlie. Leila ran into the scene, pulled up Claudia and forced her a little further away from the fight.

Lee kept the gun aimed between Kurt's eyes.

'You have no bullets,' Kurt said, in a remarkably calm tone of voice.

Lee remembered that he was, indeed, out of ammunition, only wearing his gun for reasons of fashion. The gun barrel remained levelled. At stressful times such as the one he was involved in, he always thought what his father would have done in the same spot – no doubt Kurt would already be unconscious.

'Wait right fucking there!' Lee shouted at Kurt.

Through calls of caution, and the grasping hands of Claudia, Lee ran to his bedroom, discarding his Colt as he went, and retrieved his Glock 9mm from Claudia's bunk.

Acting on auto-pilot, he was back in front of Kurt within thirty to forty seconds, aiming the loaded automatic at exactly the same spot.

Gloria, disturbed from her slumbers, popped her head around the corner of the bunkhouse, before quickly withdrawing it.

'Lee!' shouted Jon at the top of his voice, as he arrived to see the drama. 'Lee!'

In little groupings of people around the fort the sole topic of conversation inevitably was: how did they move on after something like that?

Leila stood with Charlie up on the west wall, even though they couldn't see the river.

'Oh, my God, Charlie. That's really bad. I can't believe how bad that is.'

'I agree, kid. Have a fight by all means, but don't threaten to shoot the man in the head.'

'What do we do now?'

'I don't know. Keep them apart, I suppose. Pray for the boat to come.'

'Charlie, I'm on Lee's side, of course. But that was just silly to do that.'

He put an arm around her shoulders and she was pleased to be hugged.

'On a lighter note,' he said. 'It's great that you got together with Jon. I said it all along.'

She cringed into his shoulder. 'Oh, Charlie.'

Down in the cookhouse, Jon was in conversation with Devin, who was outraged over Lee's show of aggression. Jon was less upset, but still disturbed by developments. Neither man could decide what was to happen next, though they were in agreement that the atmosphere had hit rock bottom.

There was a mothers' meeting in Prodilyn and Gloria's office. The two women had the chairs, Andy and Kevin were standing, while Kurt sat on the floor with his back to the wall, playing solemnly with the tongues of his boots. Kevin's rage had only just subsided – he had driven the conversation on what should be done with Lee. First he had suggested house arrest, then banishment, at the very least they should disarm the man. Andy had very calmly pointed out that most of them had been routinely armed for over a month.

Clearly there was no easy answer in such a small world. Kurt was in the wrong, and so was Lee. Basically, it was a social calamity for the group.

Gloria, for her part, had had a brief hysterical rant against Lee and Claudia, without offering any suggestions, before lapsing back into silence. Prodilyn remained constant throughout, watching the maelstrom whirl around her.

In the bunkhouse, Lee paced his room, while Claudia sat on the top bunk, stunned and unhappy.

'Why did I do that?' Lee berated himself. 'I was never going to kill him, so why do that? I should have beaten the crap out of him, instead.'

'It's done now,' said Claudia.

'So what, we sit in here for five months? Or we have a shit time out there every day. What a fuck-up.'

'Lee, tomorrow there might be a way forward. Charlie and Phil, as well as Jon will be trying to work it out. Come here.'

He sulked a moment longer, then went across to lean on

her legs and let her cradle his head.

'Sorry, babe,' he said.

'I know. I know.'

Michelle managed to calm her husband down, and they put together an evening meal which Leila and Jon distributed to the two camps, as well as to Phil who had withdrawn to the jail again.

Leila had visited Lee and Claudia earlier in the afternoon, offering her support and keeping them up to date on recent discussions. There were hugs all round.

'Jon's with you, as well,' she had told them. 'And Charlie.'

After she had left them, Claudia commented, 'It seems we're split into cliques again, just like the shopping mall.'

Lee had shrugged, 'Let's see what the morning brings.'

That night, Doc said something along those same lines to the few people with him in the cookhouse. Leland lay on the chaise longue, Charlie sat at the piano without touching the keys, while Devin and Michelle sat together eating cookies. Doc got to his feet, 'Right, y'all, I'm going to bed. Enough drama for one day.'

The morning brought more fog. People began to stir, and as they went about their routines they realised it was ridiculous that they were hoping not to bump into Lee or Kurt. Feeling absolutely silly themselves, Claudia checked the way was clear before she and Lee went to the latrines together.

Most of the people gathered in the cookhouse. Charlie called for attention, wanting to offer a solution to the situation. The only ones not in attendance, apart from Lee and Claudia, were Andy, Leland and Kurt.

'Listen up, please,' said Charlie. 'May I make a suggestion? Why don't we gather up all the weapons, period and modern? Disarm everyone. Then, when guns are out of the equation, we can see whether Lee and Kurt can get by in here.'

'Well said!' called Michelle.

The idea seemed sensible enough, thought Doc, although he was reluctant to give up his pistol, and doubted whether some of the others not there would go for it, either. He saw that all around him were nodding. What a relief. Yes, that's the way forward. Well done, Charlie.

Then suddenly gunshots rang out in the compound. The only person not to jump up in shock was Prodilyn.

Kevin and Charlie were bold enough to investigate, walking briskly out into the opaque, foggy morning, others gathering on the boardwalk behind them. Jon decided to catch the two men up, hugging Leila before jogging after them.

Two noises were homed in on, both disturbing in their own way. Halfway between the jail and the bunkhouse there came a groaning and a gurgling. Kevin stumbled forward onto a prostrate Kurt, the one making the pain noise.

'Christ, it's Kurt!' shouted Kevin, kneeling down. 'He's been shot!'

A cursory check by Kevin found gunshot wounds to Kurt's left arm, both upper and forearm. The man was extremely distressed, but otherwise not hurt in any other place. Hurrying over, Charlie came across the source of the gurgling noise. Leland lay motionless on his back, his hands to his throat, blood bubbling up through his fingers from a gunshot to the neck.

'Oh, fucking hell,' said Charlie, immediately attempting to press a handkerchief onto Leland's throat.

Completing the scene in the gloom, Jon screamed out for help. 'Doc! Doc!'

Everyone approached. Doc ran forward, glanced at Kurt, before giving his total attention to Leland.

The three men first on the spot, Kevin, Charlie and Jon, stood together witnessing the tragedy. It was Kevin who stood on something in the mud. He bent and picked it up, holding out his hand to show Lee's 9mm Glock automatic to the other two.

TWENTY-SEVEN

Despite the valiant efforts of Doc, Leland died out there in the fog.

Most people remained with him, in total shock, Michelle and Gloria crying their eyes out, while Kurt was moved to the cookhouse for treatment on his wounds. Once Doc decided his patient was stable, he left him with Charlie and Prodilyn and returned to Leland, where he firmly gave instructions for the body to be covered up and moved inside. Andy, lately arrived on the spot, took charge of that task, roping in Devin for help. Feeling quite numb, Devin embraced his wife before saying he was ready.

There were ten people standing in a semi-circle around Leland's body: Doc, Gloria, Michelle, Devin, Andy, Kevin, Jon, Leila and Phil, and a curious zombie. Andy looked slowly to his left, then did a double-take. Gloria was another to spot the intruder, virtually collapsing in terrified histrionics. Everyone scattered in alarm, nearly all were still unaware of what was happening. Andy drew his gun and shot the zombie through the mouth. Michelle screamed, Devin grabbed for her. The zombie crumpled.

'Jon, Kevin!' called Andy. 'Zombies in the compound!

Come with me. Everyone else into the cookhouse.'

As all the others rushed for the safety of the cookhouse, the three gunmen stalked around in the fog. 'Stay close,' called Andy. They moved towards the stable block, because of the recent incursion from that area. At the wall, where the fire had damaged the wood, they found the upturned wagon had been edged inwards by the force of zombies at the opening. There was no obvious threat inside, so they moved in and took turns blasting the mass of zombie flesh plugging the gap. When the pressure had been released, they put the wagon back in place.

'What now?' asked Kevin. 'We can't check the whole compound in this fog. Maybe it was just the one that got through.'

'Let's get into the cookhouse,' said Jon. 'Re-evaluate there.'

Andy accepted that. 'Okay. Retire to the cookhouse.'

'What about Leland?' asked Kevin.

'We collect him on the way,' said Andy.

They did just that, Kevin and Jon carrying the body while Andy provided cover. Into the cookhouse they made a gruesome entry, prompting further tears from the females so disposed. Devin led them to a neutral place between the kitchen and the stores where they laid down Leland's body. Once it was covered with a sheet they all sighed in relief and joined the others.

Andy explained what they had done, and how difficult it would be to sweep the fort in the foggy conditions. 'Let's just catch our breath,' he said. 'Then we can think about checking for other zombies, and reinforcing the hole in the wall.'

Devin handed out soft drinks. Nobody was speaking.

'Lee and Claudia are still out there,' pointed out Leila.

'Yes, they are, young lady,' said Phil. He was on his feet, apparently indignant. It was like he was standing for office, that he had found a cause at last. 'Lee should be taken into custody.'

'Too right,' put in Kevin. 'A citizen's arrest.'

'Now just a minute,' objected Jon.

Charlie stood up to add his opinion to the argument. It was then that Lee and Claudia entered the cookhouse, and all eyes turned to them.

'We heard gunfire,' said Claudia, protectively holding on to Lee.

'Arrest him!' screamed Gloria, standing up and encroaching into Claudia's personal space. 'He killed Leland. Arrest the murdering bastard!'

Claudia no longer had hold of her boyfriend, as she decked Gloria with one punch to the left cheekbone. Pandemonium erupted, people went for Lee, while others tried to stop any such action. Guns were drawn by Andy and Kevin. Phil stood before Lee, then he thought better of the idea and left it to the younger men.

Doc and Charlie were trying to bring some calm to the proceedings, but it had gone too far. Lee was held firmly from behind by Kevin. Lee would have immediately attempted to extricate himself, but with Andy's pistol in his face he decided it was best not to. Claudia had flown into a rage, attempting to scratch Andy's face, then trying to attack Prodilyn as she got involved.

Eventually, Leila and Charlie managed to control Claudia.

255

Lee was bundled out of the cookhouse and forced towards the jail.

'Claudia,' said Charlie. 'Just let it happen for now. Leland's been shot dead, Kurt wounded. When the madness calms down we'll all deal with it better.'

'That's right, honey,' said Leila.

Lee was thrown into a cell in the back of the jail, and locked in. He knew it was pointless to rant and rave at his captors, so, as he watched Andy, Kevin and Phil conspire over what procedure to adopt for holding him there, he sat down on the bed and tried to keep calm.

After about forty minutes in pokey, Lee was beginning to seethe with fury. He knew Claudia would be fighting his corner alongside his friends, but things looked bad. *Leland dead.*

Only Phil had stayed to watch over him. He had one of the Winchester rifles with him. There was zero conversation. There was no John Wayne banter with the prisoner. Lee thought Phil had lost his mind, gone stir crazy, believing he was some kind of US Marshall back in the Old West.

Finally, Lee received a visitor. He was hoping for his lawyer, but had to settle for Charlie.

'You can have five minutes with the prisoner,' said Phil.

For the first time in the fort, Charlie lost his temper, big time, facing down the other man. 'What's rattled your cage, Phil!? Are you fucking enjoying this madness!?'

'No, I'm not enjoying a young American boy being gunned down by a psychotic Englishman.'

'Have you ever heard of a small thing called proof, Phil?'

Shaking his head in dismay, Charlie walked through to converse with Lee.

'How's Claudia?' Lee asked, immediately.

'Your young lady is still apoplectic with rage, but Leila is keeping her under control. We're trying to get a handle on this, Lee. This is heavy shit, you know. Listen, I'm an ex-copper. I wouldn't have asked you this without a solicitor, but did you take a few pot shots at Kurt?'

'And leave my gun at the scene, Charlie?'

'That's what I thought. You've just got to be patient, lad. You know what these Americans are like when it comes to law and order. We've just got to wait for the boat, alert the authorities and get this matter put into official hands.'

Lee didn't say anything. He knew he just had to sweat it out.

'Claudia will come and see you soon. We'll get food out here. Just sit tight.'

They shook hands before Charlie departed the jail.

Claudia couldn't take any more dirty looks from Prodilyn and Gloria, or, for that matter, no looks at all from the other people in the cookhouse, so retreated to her room, where she was joined by Leila, Jon and Charlie for a council of war. They discussed taking on the other group immediately, releasing Lee and demanding that someone go for help. Once again, Charlie urged caution, pointing out that emotions were running high at that moment in time. Plus, surely the boat was due any day.

Claudia had calmed down from the initial shock of Lee being accused in that kangaroo court fashion. Leila had explained to her that Charlie was an ex policeman, so she was happy to have him on her side, and would listen to his advice.

'But I want to see Lee, now,' said Claudia, stepping into her boots from her position of sitting on the lower bunk.

'We'll all go,' said Jon.

There came a knock at the door. Everyone looked at everyone else. Jon let go of Leila's hand to go and open it, allowing Doc to enter.

'Hello, sorry to interrupt,' said Doc.

'Come in, Doc,' said Claudia. 'You know you're welcome here.' She finished tying her laces and got to her feet. 'Sit down, why don't you?'

'No, I'll stand, thank you. How are you bearing up? Okay? Listen, um, something's been nagging away at the back of my mind for a little while. Something Andy said.'

Charlie and Jon exchanged a look.

'I didn't pick up on it at the time,' continued Doc. 'I think I was lost in thoughts of my wife. Anyway, it was only a split second, but Andy addressed Prodilyn as Mrs Hester. I remember you mentioning that name from your previous event.'

Claudia had already sat down again on hearing that Prodilyn was Michael Hester's widow. Leila joined her and they clasped hands.

'Hester?' said Jon, piecing it together. 'The man who organised the thing in England was called Hester, right?'

'Damn right,' said Claudia, her mind racing again, a rush of adrenalin coursing through her body.

She and Leila made noises and gestures to each other, and blowing out of cheeks, trying to get a handle on what they were looking at. Could it possibly be? Could it all be an elaborate, insane game of revenge?

'That evil bitch,' said Claudia. 'I can't believe this. This isn't happening.'

Charlie had taken to pacing the room. Doc and Jon watched him walk by their faces. He stopped so suddenly, they all looked to him. 'I think Andy took Lee's gun and used it to fire at Kurt – to incriminate Lee. Leland was just in the wrong place at the wrong time.'

Jon swore to himself. He knew he shouldn't have come on this madcap caper. He suddenly needed to breathe deeply, looking at his feet; then he realised Leila was watching him, so he put his shoulders back and thought, fuck it, I'm here, there's been a horrible crime carried out, and I'm going to stand up against that. He gave Leila a wink.

'We'll have to act,' said Charlie. 'They might think Doc is in the dark. They might be under the impression they can take their time.'

'To do what?' asked Doc.

'Who knows what's in their heads?' continued Charlie. 'I suggest we strike out of here tonight. Before they realise.'

'And go where?' asked Leila.

'Who's they?' asked Jon.

Charlie counted off on his fingers. 'Prodilyn, Andy, surely Gloria as well. I would think one more male. And where do we go, Leila? Barbra's ranch to start with. Get her to call the police.'

'What if she's in on it?' asked Jon.

'How do we get there?' asked Leila.

'The horses, Leila. We ride out of here. And even if she is

part of this conspiracy, we make her call the cops. We do it for her. She won't be expecting us showing up there.'

Claudia had held her tongue until then. She got to her feet again. She looked first at Doc. 'Doc, are you with us?'

'I, erm, yes. I'm with you.'

'Then Charlie, I think it's best we leave. If you, Jon and Doc will release Lee, me and Leila will make the horses ready.'

Charlie nodded. 'When it's good and dark we'll make our move. Right now everyone, time out here. I think we should work through a plan of action.'

Due to the threat of possible zombies inside the fort, all Claudia's group accompanied her to visit Lee in the jail. On arrival, Claudia completely ignored Phil and skipped through to hold Lee through the bars of his cell. Phil stood looking at the four people surrounding him, but didn't say a word.

Lee kissed Claudia. 'Don't worry,' he told her. 'It's just a misunderstanding. Anyway, you must be used to visiting people in prison, from what you've told me about your family.'

She giggled through her emotion. She kissed him again.

'Lee,' she whispered, 'now stop joking and listen. We're getting out of here tonight. On the horses.'

'What?'

'Prodilyn, Lee. Prodilyn is Michael Hester's widow.' She paused for that to sink in with him. 'This is all her doing. This is all meant to end badly, Lee. Listen to me, Charlie, Jon and Doc are going to come in here for you tonight. Be ready to go.'

'Fucking hell, babe. I'm so sorry for getting you into this. I promised to look after you from the first minute to the last.'

'And you will, darling. Just be ready tonight.'

'How did you find out about her?'

'That doesn't matter now. I love you so very much, do you know that. So very much.'

'I love you, too.'

They kissed again, then she left him, just as Phil was about to state some rule about visiting rights he had just made up. Phil watched them file out into the fog, had a look for rogue zombies, then closed the door.

In the cookhouse, rational argument was doing battle with jingoistic fervour against the "English" group. Michelle was trying to come to terms with the legal ramifications of locking up Lee, while Gloria was shouting that it was the least that should be done to him. Devin had cooled his heels and was siding with his wife.

'He threatened him with a smuggled in automatic pistol!' shouted Gloria. 'And then he went and used it!'

'But we don't know that for sure,' said Devin.

'Who else could it be?' asked Gloria. 'A robotic zombie?'

Andy, as always the man with the expressionless face, sat quietly nearby.

TWENTY-EIGHT

Early evening, Doc entered the cookhouse. Everyone looked at him as he stood there, judging whether he was part of the "English" group or not. But Doc was American and, besides, as a medical practitioner, he should be considered neutral.

Doc went over and checked on Kurt's condition, as the Swede reclined on the chaise-longue. Michelle got Doc a drink of cocoa and placed it down beside him.

'There you are, Doc,' she said.

'Thank you, Michelle. Oh, Michelle, the two men in the jail, Phil and Lee, they must need some food.'

'I've just come back from there, Doc. Two nice meals on trays. All's well, in that regard, at least.

Doc nodded and watched her move off. Then he stood, tasted his cocoa, looked about him. He walked over to stand between where Andy and Kevin were sitting, addressing them together, 'We really should put Leland's body elsewhere. Perhaps the office cabin.'

Andy looked up at Doc, with light from a nearby kerosene lamp flickering on his face. 'I'll see to it immediately, Doc.'

'Thank you.'

Doc went off to sit in his usual spot near the window. Actually, his zombie novel was there, but he was too stressed to pick it up. Instead, he listened to the sporadic chatter in the cookhouse. Gloria seemed to have burned herself out on the subject of retribution, talking instead about something called Pinterest, a site to do with organising the things you like, which she used to do, back in the days when there was internet.

Then Doc caught a snippet of something between Andy and Prodilyn. 'Should I relieve Judge Phil?' asked Andy.

'No, he's happy out there. Doing something productive for a change.'

'I'll move Leland now.'

Doc followed Andy to where Leland's covered corpse lay.

'May I help you, Andy?'

'Sure.'

They picked up Leland and carried him outside into the dark, heading towards Prodilyn's office.

'Are we safe out here?' asked Doc.

'Me and Kevin checked everywhere two hours ago. While you were with the others.'

'No danger, then. Good. Did I hear you call Phil a judge?'

Andy didn't answer immediately, just a lumbering shape six feet or so away from Doc. Then he answered as if he didn't think it mattered any more.

'Man was a judge in Connecticut for a dozen years or so. Then his wife died, he fell apart, then the world exploded, really fell apart. Don't suppose there's much call for judges when they haven't even got a police force.'

'Well, that's a surprise. It must have been hard for him.'

'Too right. A judge, down to working in a coffee shop.'

Charlie's plan didn't stretch as far as waiting for the early hours – when the other group would be asleep – as soon as darkness dropped into the fog, they were under way. Claudia and Leila, who had spent a few hours making bridles out of rope they had collected from the stables, packed their personal items into their coat pockets and left the building. Ever practical, they visited the latrines first, before approaching the horses in their makeshift stable, where they spent some time apologising for disturbing them, and soothing them, in anticipation for the imminent departure.

Jon, Doc and Charlie, also in possession of a length of rope, wrapped up warm for the journey and headed for the jail. As planned, they barged straight in, finding Phil in the action of jumping from his chair, half asleep. Within two seconds they had him down, muffled with a hand to the mouth. With the rope they quickly bound his hands and feet, and gagged him with a piece of torn from the bed linen. Jon tried to stuff some of the material into Phil's mouth, but Doc ordered that they only cover the outside, and checked that the man's nasal passages were clear to breathe before they turned their attention to Lee.

The key to the cell was easily found and Lee was liberated, amid hushed thanks and acknowledgements. Lee immediately set about preparing himself for the journey. He put on Phil's coat, and then, as an afterthought, strapped on Leland's gun belt which had been left there earlier in the day by Andy. Having his hand on the gun made him feel like Billy the Kid, breaking out of jail in Lincoln County, 1881.

'Right then,' said Charlie. 'I'll go for the girls. Get the gate open and wait for us.' At the last second, Charlie picked up the Winchester which Phil had been in charge of. He looked at Lee. 'Should I take this?'

'Go for it,' answered Lee.

Doc and Jon did the work at the gate, with Lee still a little stunned to be outside. Through the darkness came the caravan of figures leading horses. It took a moment for Claudia to identify her man before she threw her arms around him.

'No time for that,' muttered Charlie. 'Mount up as we agreed.'

Claudia got on Aubrey, with Lee behind her. Leila took Ashley with Jon. Doc was on Naomi, fairly uncomfortably. Charlie rode Amelie.

They walked the horses out through the gate and followed the train track as best they could. Within moments they were clear. Jon let out a sigh of relief, Leila giggled and Charlie said, 'Hush.'

They continued steadily on, occasionally sensing zombies shuffling about in the gloom, once or twice seeing movement, but, like a battleship avoiding a blockade outside a port, they made it through without being accosted.

Lee held tight to Claudia's waist, nervous with the escape but delirious to have her smell near to him, and to be able to lose his face in her flowing hair. 'You're magnificent,' he said to her left ear.

'You know what, babe?' she replied. 'Looks like Christmas in Connecticut.'

'Sounds perfect to me.'

Gloria's face sported a massive shiner, courtesy of Claudia's right hook. It was on show to everyone at breakfast, which was a muted affair with little or no conversation. Gloria pushed her plate away from her. She looked daggers at Kevin and Andy, sitting there separately munching away without a care in the world. Prodilyn, seated to her left, had her hair pulled violently into a ponytail, making her appear pinched and uptight – not surprising, really. Gloria didn't feel like talking to her friend. She noticed that Michelle was preparing a breakfast tray for the jail.

'I'll take that across,' she called.

Andy glanced up, but didn't say anything. Michelle loaded up Gloria's arms and sent her on her way. The fog had lifted for the most part. It remained still and ghostlike. Gloria made her way towards the jail, starting to hum *The Love Boat* (probably brainwashed by Charlie's piano playing) before remembering that times were not happy enough for that kind of thing.

She was surprised to find the door wide open as she approached, and even more surprised to see a bound and gagged Phil lying on his side on the floor. She discarded the tray sideways with a loud smash and rushed in to squat down beside the man. She removed the gag, but didn't at first consider untying him. A glance about her told her the prisoner had clearly escaped. 'What the fuck have you let happen, you useless old bastard?'

Phil was physically unhurt, but in a highly distressed state following his lengthy ordeal. His lips moved but he had nothing to say to the woman.

'Well!?' she screamed at him. 'When did he go?'

'Many hours...' he managed to whisper.

Gloria slapped Phil across the face, perhaps without even knowing she was doing it. Then she stood, intending to rush to tell the others, before she decided to at least untie the man. It was a struggle, but finally she let him roll over, moaning and praying the blood would come back to his hands. Gloria ran from the jail.

She scared Michelle at the stove as she ran shouting into the cookhouse, causing Prodilyn and Kevin to jump to their feet.

'Lee's escaped!' she told them, breathlessly.

'Kevin,' said Prodilyn, 'go check on the others.'

Kevin stood up and left the building, accepting without question that he was in Prodilyn's group. Prodilyn looked furiously at Gloria, then across at Andy who remained calmly seated.

'And what have you got to say on the matter?' Prodilyn asked of Andy.

Andy declined to comment. Kevin was soon back, reporting on the others' flight on the horses.

'Where have they gone?' asked Gloria.

'The only place they know,' said Andy, 'the ranch.'

'Well?' continued Gloria, 'do we just let him get away?'

'Everyone,' called Devin. 'That might be the best outcome.'

Prodilyn spun on him. 'Shut your mouth!'

Andy got up and moved to stand in front of Prodilyn.

'Mrs Hester, do you want to chase after them?' he asked.

She answered coldly, 'Yes, Andy, I want to chase after them.'

'But how!?' cried Gloria.

Prodilyn slapped Gloria on the opposite side of her face to the bruising. Gloria just took the blow, stunned and embarrassed.

'You shut up as well,' snarled Prodilyn.

Andy was readjusting his gun belt and then finishing his coffee. 'We go on the hand cart, that's how.'

The travelling through the night was slow going. They continued following the track, hoping by sun up to get somewhere near the place to cut off towards the ranch. Lee was reminded of Kurt during the journey in, how he said it was the longest day of his life.

The pairs talked sporadically to each other; Jon to Leila, Lee to Claudia, Charlie to Doc. Jon told Leila stories of the London he used to know, and of where they would be living.

'It sounds nice,' she said, 'But...'

'But what?'

'It's a flat.'

'A nice flat.'

She patted the horse's neck. 'But where would we keep Ashley?'

'Very funny.'

'Tell me about your London friends.'

'My London friends? I lost a couple in the... you know what. There is Martin, he's a good lad. Used to be in the army, so a pub fight was always guaranteed when out with him. There's Stuart, ex fireman, and Robbie. Robbie's a bit of a joker.'

'Why, what does he do?'

'Well, I'll give you an example. When we were teenagers, we were at a Bonfire Night firework display. He offered his coat to this girl from college. She thanked him and put her arm in the sleeve, but he'd put the sleeve down the front of his trousers, so her hand went straight down there.'

Leila laughed. 'What did she do?'

'Punched him. He took it well. In fact, for a few weeks after, his catchphrase was, "I still intend to bang her".'

Lee and Claudia also talked back and forth over a shoulder, of positive things they could look forward to. They had escaped another bizarre experiment – if they heard nothing more about the killing of Leland, then they could rebuild, initially back in New Milford. Of course, they ran through Prodilyn's twisted motivations for putting the whole thing in motion at all. The enormity of it staggered them. She had provoked violence from Claudia and framed Lee for murder, all within five weeks – what would she have managed to do in the full six months?

They were both extremely relieved to be well clear of the fort, although tiredness was setting in and they still had the unknown situation at Barbra's ranch to face.

'Part of me is sad to leave,' said Claudia.

'Oh?'

'When we got to the halfway stage I was going to give you back to Leila.'

Lee laughed, as did Leila nearby, her white smile flashing in the darkness.

They lapsed into silence, with Claudia not wanting to talk about what was behind them any more, but Charlie wanted to talk about what was ahead. He turned in his saddle, let them all close up on him.

'Don't forget,' he said, 'we don't know whether Barbra is in on this thing or not. We must stick together when we get there, until I've definitely spoken to the outside world. Are we clear on that?'

They all responded in the affirmative.

The hand cart left the fort within thirty minutes of the alarm being raised. Kevin, Andy and a half-hearted Prodilyn worked the mechanism up and down, while the injured Kurt stood shotgun. Straight out of the gate they encountered three zombies. Kurt despatched them easily with his pistol, despite being in pain.

Gloria and Phil watched them go – Gloria given a mouthful of abuse by Prodilyn. She was angry to be left behind, and with Phil in a world of his own, confused to have been handed responsibility once more and then have it ripped away. He drifted off towards his jail, as more gunshots rang out.

'Fuck it!' swore Gloria, left looking for Devin to close the gate, but the cretin was hiding with his equally stupid wife. Gloria shut the gate and only just managed to lift the wooden bar into place. She was furious, to be actually left in the middle of Texas with two cooks, a nut job and a corpse. She went running after Phil.

'It's all your fault, you moron!' she screamed at him. Phil turned and looked at her as he mounted the stairs in a dream. 'You let us down with your fucking incompetence!'

Phil stood at the door to his jail. He was actually rocking back and forth slightly, so that when Gloria came to shout, up close and personal, he even moved nearer to each swear word. She was running the full gamut of estuary English right into his face, destroying him, sending him over the edge.

She gasped, distraught herself, done with him and the whole sorry mess. She was about to walk away, to rest, to eat, to think of a way out of there, when suddenly this old man had her by the throat. *He's actually trying to strangle me*, she thought, her knees initially weakening, then flailing in panic as his grip tightened. All she could see were his eyes, expressionless, dead – his face was unimportant in that moment.

Perhaps Phil wasn't aware of what he was doing – in court it would be called temporary insanity. He did know that the horrible woman was changing colour, knew that her nails were scratching at his cheeks and neck. And then he was free of her and he stood there alone, breathing hard, rocking back and forth again. After a moment he looked down for Gloria at his feet, but saw only a square gap in the floorboards, with a rope swinging through the centre of it. He staggered sideways, down the steps. Somehow he had fixed the noose around Gloria's neck, pulled the lever and... He sank to his knees in the mud. The shadow of Gloria's twitching legs played over his face.

TWENTY-NINE

In the breaking dawn, the six bedraggled riders were off drifting to the east of the ranch, and were lucky to be found by two of Barbra's cowboys, who led them in. Barbra ran outside to meet them, issuing instructions to her staff as the surprise visitors were all helped down from the horses and taken inside. While the others drank lemonade and ate sandwiches, Charlie took a shocked Barbra into a corridor for a conference. From where he sat in the ranch house kitchen, Jon could watch the conversation, reporting back that Barbra seemed to be taking it with all intense seriousness.

Leila leant into Jon and he embraced her. Claudia smiled at Lee. It felt good to be at the ranch. It was also a little comical, because they were being watched from across the room by two separate family groups who were in the middle of their dude ranch vacations, eyeing the strangers, unsure if this had been mentioned by the travel agent. There were also a couple of cowboys and a chef looking at them from behind the staff partition.

'It feels a bit like the ending of the film *Southern Comfort*,' Lee said to Jon.

'I'm not familiar with that one,' replied Jon.

'The National Guard characters have been hunted through the Louisiana swamps by Cajun locals. They reach safety at the end, but they're not sure how safe they really are.'

'Lee, stop it,' admonished Claudia.

'Sorry.'

Charlie returned to them and assured them that he had spoken to the outside authorities, and that everything would be all right. Jon looked at Charlie before sharing a nervous giggle with Lee.

'What's funny?' asked Charlie.

'Ignore them,' said Claudia. 'They're just two silly boys.'

'Oh, right. We might as well get our heads down for a few hours. Barbra says we can go into her private quarters, due to there being guests here.'

Leila yawned, agreeing for all of them what a good idea that was.

Claudia and Lee walked hand in hand after the others. They were given a little room with wood panelling and an uncomfortable looking bed. The carpet was bright red and there was a square television set with actual antennae sticking out of it.

'Good God,' said Claudia, 'we've stepped back into the 1970's.'

'It'll do for a couple of hours.'

She kissed him hard on the mouth, their bodies closing the door.

'You stink,' she said.

'I love your foreplay technique.'

'Boy, if you think anything's happening right now, you're sorely mistaken. We need to rest, we might have a long journey out of here.'

'Promise me something. We'll never come to Texas ever again.'

'Fine by me.'

It was mid afternoon by the time they all awoke and came back together in the kitchen. First up, Charlie had made coffee for them all. Lee took his cup to a window, looking out on a bright sunny day, with horses in a paddock, but no cowboys or dudes about.

'You know those people we met in here earlier?' he said. 'They're probably going to be moving cattle to Oklahoma or somewhere. Shall we join them? We might as well get something out of this trip.'

He had five aghast faces looking at him, which made him laugh. Claudia got up and kissed him.

'I'm going to say goodbye to the horses,' she said, putting on her leather coat. 'Come along?'

'No, I'll watch you from the step. Make sure to give them my love. Especially to Aubrey, she's a good old girl.'

He followed her outside and watched her walking towards the corral where she had been told the horses were. 'You've got a sexy walk,' he called after her. She waggled her behind for him.

Lee leant on a post, sipping his coffee. He could hear Leila and Jon giggling back inside, but then she was there alongside him. He remembered Claudia saying how she planned to give him back to Leila, and he smiled to himself.

'Hi, you,' he said.

'Hi, yourself.'

Then she surprisingly hugged him with all her strength. After she finally released him, he asked, 'What was that for?'

'That's in case we never see each other again after today.'

It was then that he noticed his Glock 9mm sticking out of her belt. 'Christ, Leila, what are you doing with that?'

'Jon picked it up in the jail. I made him give it to me. You don't mind, do you?'

'I suppose not. Just be careful. And, Leila, listen, I'll always remember that hug. But, aren't you booked in for the third instalment of this madness?'

He expected her to laugh – instead, she was pointing out into the distance, to the afternoon's glare.

'What?' he asked, following her stare.

'There.'

Lee saw four far-off figures approaching slowly on foot, just to the right of the barn to which the corral was attached. 'Tell the others. Go!'

Lee set off running towards where Claudia would be. He saw her between horizontal wooden fence bars and called out to her.

'What is it?' she asked, as he got to her.

'Get back to the ranch house, now!'

'Lee, you're scaring me. What's wrong?'

'They're here.'

'Oh, God.'

He pulled Claudia by the arm, propelling her in the direction of the ranch house, but she stopped again at the sight of Jon, Leila and Charlie hurrying towards them.

'Is it true?' asked Jon.

Lee pointed. 'They're approaching on foot from over

there.'

'Shit! What do we do?'

They saw Kurt first, to the left of his own group. The answer as to what to do seemed to come naturally to them somehow – they spread out to face the developing threat. Lee again made an effort to get Claudia far behind him. Then he alternated his looks between Jon to his left, Leila to his right and Charlie further beyond her, with the appearance of Kevin, Andy and then Prodilyn alongside Kurt. Prodilyn carried one of the Winchester rifles. She and her people looked exhausted, but they were clearly conferring as they walked closer and then they themselves spread out.

Lee looked back at a very frightened Claudia. Then he checked on Leila. Her hat was on, and she was leaning slightly forward. *Good God*! thought Lee, she was thinking of drawing his Glock on the other group.

What could only be described as a stand-off quickly developed out there in the sun. There were quick glances up and down Lee's line. Charlie had the Winchester out in front of him. Doc had moved his coat aside, astonishing himself with how calm he felt. Jon was the one in a panic, asking, 'What's going down here, people? Fucking hell, what are we doing here?'

On the other side, Kevin was thinking much the same thing, looking to his side for guidance. It was Kurt, sweating and in distress from his wounds, who set off the chain of events. He drew on Doc and fired. Doc responded. Charlie fired his rifle. Andy was quick off the mark, too. Noise and smoke exploded in the corral, horses whinnied. Doc and Kurt both missed with their shots.

Lee squatted and fired, Prodilyn got a round off, Kevin simply ran for his life. Leila fired the Glock twice in quick succession, hitting Kevin in both legs, by absolute pure chance, causing him to collapse face first into the dust. Charlie cocked the rifle and fired again. Prodilyn, the determined bitch that she was, was firing and cocking her Winchester as she side-stepped to her left.

Jon, terrified almost out of his mind, gave out a banshee scream as he fired at the hunched over figure of Andy. Then he screamed for real as one of Andy's shots hit him in the shoulder, dropping him backwards. Leila fired several rounds at Andy in response, but a great deal of smoke obscured the view of how successful she had been – anyway, there were no more shots from Andy. Leila ran to care for Jon.

Doc, down to his last bullet, advanced on Kurt. Kurt fired and missed. Doc fired and shot Kurt through the head. Doc stared at what he had done, astonished, shattered. Then he turned away into a coughing fit.

Lee cried out, wounded in the right side. Charlie's target now was Prodilyn. They were exchanging shots. Lee managed to compose himself, followed Prodilyn's path, and shot her in the left side of her torso. She collapsed in a heap.

The dust continued to drift about them. Those still standing remained still. Lee shared looks with Charlie, then Doc, the two of them without a scratch between them. Then he took in the sight of Leila cradling Jon by the shoulders.

'He's all right!' shouted Leila, grinning broadly. 'He's going to be all right!'

The scene cleared a little. Still with his pistol extended, although he thought it might be empty by then, Lee assessed the threat in front of them. Kevin was squealing in pain, clearly out of the game. Kurt was stone dead on the ground. Andy was dying badly from a shot to the guts, and Prodilyn was mortally wounded also, bleeding out from the chest wound, lying on her side. Lee tried to come to terms with what had just happened, with the massive adrenalin rush which had stormed his body – he breathed deeply, let everything almost calm down into place again. He looked at the main enemy once more, just to be sure. Andy was clearly done-for. Prodilyn's beautiful face lay on her left arm, staring at them, her eyes blinking once or twice. The pool of blood before her continued to spread. Then her eyes closed.

Lee stumbled backwards, feeling the pain of his wound for the first time, wanting to just hold the love of his life, Claudia, to take her away from that place. 'Claudia,' he called.

Claudia was down on the ground.

'Claudia!' screamed Lee, rushing to her side.

He slid his legs under her head and cupped her face. Claudia was lifeless, shot once just under the chin and once in the chest, where Lee's right hand settled on a blood stain. Doc and Charlie nervously moved nearer. Leila settled Jon on his back before crossing the gap, to stand horrified at the sight before her.

Lee lowered his head to press his face gently against Claudia's cheek, and just howled with utter, utter despair.